WHAT'S
FOR
DINNER?

USA TODAY BESTSELLING AUTHOR
N GRAY

Also by N Gray

The Dana Mulder Suspense Series

Nightcrawler

Deadly Pattern

Devil Mountain

Chasing Evil

My first book is dedicated to my family, for all your love and support.

And to my mother....

Vinci Books

vinci-books.com

Published by Vinci Books Ltd in 2026

1

Copyright © N Gray 2017

A CIP catalogue record for this book is available from the British Library.
Paperback ISBN: 9781036702540

The EU GPSR authorised representative is Logos Europe, 9 rue Nicolas Poussion, 17000 La Rochelle, France
contact@logoseurope.eu

Appetizer: Too Late

Gavin feels a slight jerk and a tug; the darkness brightens the moment whatever was covering him gets yanked off. Now awake, Gavin focuses on the moving fluorescent lights, but the continuous up-and-down motion makes him queasy, so he closes his eyes for a second. To alleviate the burning sensation around his sockets, he blinks vigorously to bring back some moisture then squints at the moving lights.

When he tries to ask the person pushing him where he is going, he can't find his voice. Double metal doors come into view, and they pass through into a large, dim room he doesn't recognize. He stops, and the person pushing him comes into his line of sight. It's a nurse. Without saying a word or glancing at him, she pulls him right up against a metal shelf, locks the wheels in place and leaves.

Confused as to why the nurse has abandoned him and why she hasn't explained anything, he tries to call out to the whispers outside the double doors, but again he can't make a sound. Gavin's head has limited movement, so he strains his eyes as far as he can. To his right are the tops of double-

1

frosted windows; to his left is a clock above a sterile basin where the standard pink hand sanitizer is fitted against the wall; and in front of him are the top three rows of metal shelves with their doors still open. Right above, the paint of the ceiling is pale, chipped white.

———

He closes his eyes. What was he doing before the bright lights woke him? Nancy was sitting next to him in the car, he was driving, and she had her hand over his, her smile full of sympathy. The Okinawa meeting had happened the day before, so today must be Friday, but is it morning or evening? Gavin widens his eyes and notices a small crack in the left-hand corner of the ceiling. Nancy kissed his forehead while he lay in a bed similar to the one on which he is lying now, although it wasn't as hard or as cold. It was a crisp white bed, the linen freshly bleached. Anxiety floods through him as he remembers the pimple-faced teenage doctor inserting a drip into his hand, then the cool white liquid coursing through his veins and then...nothing. Now here he is, lying on a cold, hard bed. Why isn't he in the ward with the other patients? Why aren't there doctors surrounding him, informing him of his procedure...the procedure.

He was booked for one of those procedures to open his stubbornly clogged veins, to fix his broken heart.

The rest of the lights flicker on, the double doors open and close, and someone is moving around. Gavin tries to scream: 'Help! Please help me.' But his mouth won't move, no sound comes out, and nothing escapes him. The person whistles then clangs something against doors. Water splashes.

Out the corner of his eye Gavin glimpses a teenage boy with earphones. The boy doesn't look at him either while he wrings water from his mop into the trolley then starts cleaning the floor while humming. Gavin tries to get his attention by moving his hand, but still there is nothing. Scared and frustrated, Gavin swallows at the lump choking him, and his tears are frozen. Unable to move or talk, Gavin can only stare as his eyes cloud over. What is wrong with him? Why doesn't anyone look at him? Why doesn't anyone talk to him, and why hasn't he seen a doctor who can explain what has happened? For that matter, why is he lying in this room, naked, able to feel yet unable to move?

Then, there's his business and all the proposals he still needs to get through. Those greedy shareholders can use the fact that he is lying here, not able to do his job, to besmirch his reputation once and for all and gain a majority vote. If only Gavin brought his sons into the business when they first asked. They could've helped him; they would've maintained his position. Even though they are young, they will learn; he will teach them. When he gets out of here, he will take the time to teach them everything so that they can take over.

And Nancy, his loving beautiful wife. He closes his eyes again and recalls the day he met her while hiking on the Crescent Meadows trail through Eldorado Canyon, her laughing at him when he tripped and fell in the mud; her emerald eyes teasing him when they were eventually introduced. He proposed to her on the same trail a year later, and when his company was making enough money, they eloped to Hawaii. Two years later their twin boys were born: Matthew and Michael. The wonderful memories of his family flood him, but others boil to the surface as well. His constant burning need for his company to succeed and

3

for his family to never go without, but that didn't leave him with much time for them. The late nights at the office, the yelling, the heartbroken tears…and the broken promises. All the broken promises.

Gavin closes his eyes and starts to pray, to be able to move and get out of this place and join his family. He will do anything, just as long as he can be with them again; he will do anything and everything if only he can get out. Nobody answers him.

———

The boy heads in Gavin's direction and mops underneath him. Tongue out, half-biting, half-sucking, he scrubs with the mop for a few seconds on the same spot, and when he is satisfied, he moves the mop from side to side in wider strokes. The smell of formaldehyde becomes apparent the closer the boy comes to Gavin, and burns deep in his nostrils. The entire time that he has been cleaning, the boy has not looked at him, not once. Unnerved, Gavin wants to grab hold of the boy's shirt and let him know he needs help, but his hand isn't responding; it's possible that the anesthesia hasn't worn off yet. That must be it.

The boy sterilizes the floor near Gavin then moves on to the next section, blissfully humming along with his tunes. Being someone who appreciates the cost of time, means Gavin has no time to waste. Lying here, unable to move, is wasting his time. He could be with his family right now, laughing, sharing a meal, embracing his wife. Instead he is stuck, unable to move, unable to speak, unable to do anything. All he wants to do is get out of here and he is willing to do whatever is asked if he can just be with them.

He thinks of all the promises he made of his time, and

how he broke every one of them. Even while on vacation, he would work while his family frolicked about in the sea. Everyone was happy and full of smiles, while Gavin would be on his laptop and moan at anyone who dare disturb him. Nobody dared.

Nancy held their little family together while he provided for them. She would wait for him to get home after a long day, always greet him with a smile then plant a loving kiss on his cheek, always; while Gavin would brush past her to get back to work in his home office.

A stab of guilt twists its blade inside his chest.

Nancy would arrange the boys' birthday parties then give excuses when their daddy would be late. She would give them a kiss and say, 'Daddy will come as soon as he can'. She is his world and he never reciprocated.

Another stab of guilt and his chest twists and tightens, squeezing a little more out of him.

The pain is too much for him, and a lonely, icy tear escapes, slides down the right side of his face.

———

"Joey! What in God's name are you doing in here?" Dr. Orion asks a little too loudly as he bursts through the swinging doors.

Joey looks up at Dr. Orion, pulls his earphones off, and says, "What's wrong, uncle? You said I must mop, so I'm mopping."

"I said mop where the blood is. Do you see any blood in here? The blood is out there in the other room where I was working." Dr. Orion points to the next set of doors across the hallway.

"Sheesh! Sorry! I will go there now."

Joey dunks his mop in the trolley, pushes it through the double doors and disappears into the next room.

Looking back at his uncle, he smirks. "And there was blood in this room, over there in the corner by the new dead guy." He points in the deceased's direction.

"Please just go mop in the other room."

Irritated by his adolescent nephew's attitude, he goes to his desk and takes a deep breath and shakes his head at the thought of the things people do for family. He removes his white coat, places it over his chair and picks up the new folder from his 'In' tray. Dr. Orion looks over at the new arrival and sighs. This one was so young!

Dr. Orion goes over to the new body and gazes at the dead man's face, whose eyes are wide open, staring into nothing. It's not often he pities the deceased, but there is something about this one that elicits sympathy. It's odd that the man's mouth is still closed, so he places his forefinger onto the man's chin and applies pressure to see whether it's anchored, and it is. Rigor mortis has set in. He studies the man's frozen face and sees a sparkle in his right eye, shrugs and chalks it up to the anesthesia and the fact that it's possible for a man to shed a tear right before his death.

The quiet evening accentuates the ticking clock above the sterile basin; the little arm moves toward the nine. It's getting late.

Tired after his busy day, he doesn't want to start on the man's autopsy now. It can wait till tomorrow morning. Marge has prepared their anniversary dinner and wants him to get home on time.

Dr. Orion pushes the man into the refrigerator and closes the metal door.

Entree: The Villa

Beverley sits with Mark across from Mr. Hubbard, an old large wooden desk with detailed carvings between them, wondering in which seat her uncle sat eight days ago. The last time Bev spoke with Uncle Tim was a little more than a month ago when she asked for a loan, and he had been so excited about a new venture and promised tell her all about it upon his return. Now she is still reeling from the shock of her only uncle's passing, in addition to the run of bad luck she and Mark have experienced of late; it has become all too much.

Even focusing on Mr. Hubbard's mouth while he speaks is too much for Bev as her attention keeps wandering from Mr. Hubbard's lips to the wonderfully hand-crafted traditional masks on the wall behind him. Her attention shifts again when Mr. Hubbard moves his chair to his left and knocks the desk with his knee, the religious bobble heads shaking their disapproving heads at her. She needs to focus.

"I don't understand what you are saying, Mr. Hubbard."

Bev exhales as she stares at the large look-a-like head belonging to Pope Francis, his head still wobbling.

Fighting back tears, she sips on her tea and burns her lip again. Like a child who has forgotten what her parents just warned her about, she keeps making the same mistake. If it's not the tea that keeps burning her, it's all the mistakes she keeps repeating.

"Let me rephrase it differently, which you, both of you, can understand," Mr. Hubbard replies.

His attention fixed on Bev, he continues, "Your uncle has already paid the three months' rent on the villa. Both of you are welcome to stay here – free of charge – for the duration of the three months." He grins.

Bev stares at Mr. Hubbard again. His icy blue eyes, strong jaw, olive skin, good hair and toned body don't match his name. To her he looks more like a Mr. Blake – not a Mr. Hubbard. A last name like Hubbard is best suited to round, short men with receding hairlines.

An awkward silence causes Bev to blush, and she realizes she has been staring into his cool blue eyes a little too long. He gazes back and smiles, waits for her to respond. She glances at her husband to see whether he noticed – he hasn't. Mark sits silently in his seat, fidgeting with his hands in his lap as he gazes outside at the beach and the welcoming water.

Bev responds a little awkwardly, "Uh, can we think about it? Can we discuss it first?"

"You can discuss it, but you need to decide now. If you fail to take up occupancy by tonight, you can take the hour ferry across to the mainland. And I will offer it to someone else, and they will enjoy it at your uncle's expense."

As if reading her mind, Mr. Hubbard rises. "I need to fetch something. You can discuss it with your husband while

I am out." He leaves the room and closes the door behind him.

"Well, Mark, what do you think?" Bev turns to face her husband.

Mark finally looks in his wife's direction. "Well, we don't have money. Neither of us has a job. We need a place to stay and, well, I guess a holiday would be good for us right now. Don't you think?"

"I know. I feel the same, but I just can't believe what happened to Uncle Tim, and to stay in the same place where he died, kinda creeps me out."

"Me too, but we ain't got nowhere else to go."

Bev can hear the plea in his voice. They can use these three months to figure things out.

"Okay!"

"Okay?" Mark replies more cheerfully.

She smiles back.

Mr. Hubbard enters the room with two golden writing pens, and a blade.

"Now, is that a yes I hear?"

"Yes, we will stay," Bev replies.

Mr. Hubbard nods then continues with the process.

———

Beverly and Mark finally relax once Mr. Hubbard leaves them in the privacy of their villa. They take a tour of their new residence, admire the high ceilings, the open-plan lounge with kitchenette, the large bathroom with luxurious features and two, just-as-opulent, large bedrooms. The inviting warmth of the villa calms their nerves, and they unpack their bags and settle in.

The kitchenette only provides the basics; there are two

of each (mugs, drinking glasses, knives, forks, spoons and plates); a kettle to make themselves tea or coffee (which is provided in single-serving sachets); a tiny wash basin; and a bar fridge which chills milk, two small tubs of plain yoghurt and a six-pack of the local beer. Mark takes out two beers and gives one to Bev as she exits the bedroom.

"It's so calm here, and look at that view," Mark says as they walk out onto the veranda and sit on the bench. "I could get used to this." He winks as they clink their beer bottles together.

The golden sunset casts its shimmer over the ocean, and they both smile.

"It is beautiful, Mark. We haven't stopped to enjoy a sunset like this in a while."

"No, we haven't. I didn't know this place was here, and it's only an hour flight and an hour ferry away."

"We were too busy with life and work, and for what? To be told we are no longer needed." Bev wipes away tears and downs the rest of her beer.

Mark tilts his head to the side then reaches for her hand, but doesn't touch. She stands up and goes inside.

"We need to go. It's almost seven."

———

At seven o'clock they arrive for dinner, dressed accordingly: Bev in a summer dress that accentuates her slender figure, with flat sandals, and Mark in a collar shirt, jeans and sneakers. Mr. Hubbard greets them at the door and welcomes them in. Mark allows Bev to enter the hall first; both are in awe at the size of the building with its magnificent high ceilings. Each table has a white satin tablecloth, and some tables seat two, while others seat four or eight. Fine cutlery has been placed neatly on each table.

They look at each other when they come to the same realization.

"Are we the only guests here, Mr. Hubbard?" Bev asks Mr. Hubbard before Mark can.

"For now you are." He winks at her.

Bev holds onto Mark's arm, tightening her grip as they look for a table with a view of the ocean.

Before they sit near the doorway, Mr. Hubbard calls after them, "I think it's best if the two of you sit here." He motions for them to follow him. Out of the thirty available tables, he points to a two-seater table near the open window closest to the revolving door that leads to the kitchen.

"It's easier to serve you if you sit here, plus you have the best view of the ocean," Mr. Hubbard clarifies.

Bev and Mark oblige, walk over to their assigned seats.

Mr. Hubbard continues, "For starters you have two options, escargot or prawn cocktail?"

"Those are our favorites, Mr. Hubbard. How did you know?" Bev asks as she sits down. Mark helps push in her chair. She smiles at him, but he doesn't notice.

"It is my duty to know these things, Mrs McAdams." Mr. Hubbard winks at her again, and her cheeks grow warm.

Mr. Hubbard retreats to the kitchen and moments later returns with their starters. He places the escargot in front of Mark and the prawn cocktail by Bev, which they devour. With the leftover bread, they each dip into one another's dish to taste and compare.

"Hmm, that was good." Bev moans; she can't get enough and licks sauce from her fingers.

"I didn't know I was so hungry." Mark licks his lips.

"The prawn was fresh and the sauce on top was so smooth and delicious." Bev wipes her mouth with a cloth napkin.

Mr. Hubbard returns. "Your two options for main course is a rump steak with vegetables and a sauce of your choosing or the chicken breast in lemon sauce with vegetables, with a salad to share and bread rolls." He waits patiently for their answer and begins to clear their table.

"That sounds good, I will have the chicken, please," Bev answers.

"I will have the rump steak, medium rare with a pepper sauce," Mark replies.

Twenty minutes and a glass of wine later, their main meal is placed neatly in front of them. The savory steam from their food tantalizes their taste buds. Like starving refugees they dig in. Mark cuts a slice of his juicy rump and places it on Bev's plate, and she does the same by placing a piece of her chicken on his. They enjoy every succulent bite; the chicken pulls apart easily while Bev scoops up some of the vegetables and eats. Mark doesn't need a sharp knife to cut his steak, the knife from the table glides through it effortlessly, and each bite melts in his mouth.

Bev notices Mark has sauce dripping from the corner of his mouth; she points to the corner of her mouth to show Mark he needs to wipe his mouth. He smiles and thanks her, wipes off the sauce with the napkin.

In that blissful moment, they forget about the troubles that await them back in the city.

Mark loosens his belt and says, "When last did I have to do this, Bev?"

She laughs at him. "No idea, but I am glad I chose to wear one of my loose-fitting dresses."

Mark laughs back at her.

"I feel like a teenager." She gives him a sincere smile, touches his hand.

He has almost forgotten the smoothness of her skin.

"I know!" He cocks his head, lifts her hand to his mouth, and kisses her gently. "I know!" He places her hand back on the table, still holds on.

They flicker back to reality once Mr. Hubbard starts to remove their plates.

"You didn't touch the salad or bread rolls. Was the meal too much for the two of you?"

"Yes, it was, but it was so exquisite," Bev remarks.

Mr. Hubbard smiles, then returns to the kitchen with the empty dishes.

Mark shares the remaining wine between them and they sip their last drink in silence, both lost in themselves while they gaze out onto the moonlit ocean.

Mr. Hubbard returns with a square plate, and on it are two of each bite-size tarts: creme brûlée, lemon cheesecake and chocolate mousse.

"Would you like some coffee to complement your desserts?" Mr. Hubbard asks.

"Yes please, that would be most welcomed," Bev replies while Mark nods.

Mr. Hubbard disappears into the kitchen and brings them their coffee. They enjoy it and the little tarts in silence, apart from the 'hmmm' as they bite into each sweet delicacy.

When the desserts are eaten and their coffee cups empty, they stand up. Mr. Hubbard automatically appears and promptly removes the empty dishes.

Before they reach the exit, Mr. Hubbard comes back into the hall from the kitchen. "I hope you enjoyed tonight's dinner?"

"We did, thank you. And please tell the chef he did a wonderful job."

"Certainly, but before you go, just a reminder that breakfast is at eight a.m. sharp."

They say good night then descend the dining hall steps.

They decide on a stroll along the beach, to feel the ocean lick their feet.

"It is beautiful here," Bev marvels, threads her fingers with Marks'. This brings back old memories.

"It is, and it's not that far away. I have to admit, don't you find Mr. Hubbard a little odd?" Mark replies as the lines between his eyes deepen.

"What do you mean?" Bev asks, matching his frown.

"I don't know. It's just a feeling I get whenever he is near us. He gives me the creeps."

Bev giggles. "Nonsense, Mark. I think it's your paranoia acting up again."

Mark gawks at her. "I'm just being cautious, and the doctor agreed with me the last time. If I didn't stop you in time, you would have died in that car accident." He stops, yanking her arm so hard her shoulder clicks.

"Ouch!" she cries, pulling her hand free from his. "You always do this; you turn something innocent into a malicious thing. Now come on, it's been a long day and I'm tired." She sees their villa in the distance and stomps off in that direction.

———

Mr. Hubbard stands on the dining hall veranda puffing on his cigar while watching his new guests fight in the moonlight. Let the games begin.

Bev enjoys the hot water as it massages her back and neck. Even though she is still a little annoyed with Mark for hurting her arm, the hot water relaxes her. Her mind drifts from the warm water to Mark's neurotic behavior, him yanking her arm, how angry he looked. His dark eyes, then she sees blue eyes. Mr. Hubbard's blue eyes. How he looked at her and how uncomfortable she felt. Her body heats up. It feels as he is watching her now, again, and she opens her eyes, looks behind her. It's only the white tiles. She climbs out and wraps the towel around her body, checks the empty shower again. Her brows knot together and she thinks of Mark, how he always finds a problem with something even when there is nothing to find.

Bev opens the bathroom door a little too hard and lets it thud against the wall. Then she gets dressed and climbs into bed without saying good night, closes her eyes, and thankfully there is only darkness.

Mark can hear her from where he sits, the slamming of the door, the yanking of the blinds being closed but ignores her loud movements. Another large wave crashes over a smaller one and creeps up the sand. The villa is only a few strides away from the water, and he can see every splash in the moonlight. As each wave reaches the shore and rolls back into the ocean, he thinks of each of their problems and that they don't seem to come right on any of them. Then he considers the predicament in which he finds them and he feels nauseous. A pain starts near his diaphragm, and his stomach burns. His ulcer might be acting up again. Surely we can leave anytime we want to, can't we? He is being silly, he knows they can leave when they want to, they aren't forced to stay here. He rubs his head; it has been a long day and he needs sleep. He goes back inside the villa and finds his wife in bed with her side of the room in darkness. He walks over to her and kisses her cheek; she lifts her face to his and kisses him on the lips. He smiles at her when he pulls away, kisses her again before heading to the bathroom.

———

The loud pounding wakes Mark; it's not any noise from outside but his own head. He recalls vivid dreams but doesn't remember what they were about when the pounding started. The pain and nausea are still sitting in the pit of his stomach and he turns to face Bev as she leaps out of bed.

"You're chipper this morning," he croaks.

"I feel good. I haven't slept so well in weeks. I want to go for a stroll, see what else is on this island. Do you feel like joining me?" Her beauty is radiant in the sunlight.

"I think I am rather going to lie in. I didn't sleep well." Mark squints, rolls over to face the wall.

"Suit yourself."

———

Bev pulls on the only pair of sweatpants she owns, notices the holes, but wears them anyway. She then puts on a top with a built-in bra, brushes her teeth and hair then heads for the beach, barefoot. She presses the start button on her old Stepper when she leaves the villa. Along the beach she passes nine villas similar to theirs, with a second row of smaller villas behind them. The small pier where the ferry docked to let them off is empty, and she makes a mental note to ask Hr. Hubbard how often it stops at the island or if there is a timetable she could look at. Then she passes half an old wooden boat full of twigs and broken branches near Mr. Hubbards' office and as she passes the building she can't see him there and wonders what he does all day. Lastly she passes the dining hall with its doors still closed and finally arrives back at their villa where she looks at the Stepper. The island is four miles from where she began and stopped, and it only took her an hour and a half to walk around it – at a brisk pace. Her stomach twists and pains when she enters the villa, she must have worked up quite an appetite. It is almost eight, and she needs to shower quickly if she is to be on time for breakfast.

―――――

At eight a.m. they arrive at the dining hall steps. Mark darts to their table and sits down, doesn't offer a seat for Bev. Mr. Hubbard notices their demeanor and takes the opportunity to push in Bev's seat for her, alluringly touching the back of her neck as she sits.

He begins, "Today we are serving omelet with your choice of filling."

Bev goes first. "I will have bacon and cheese with whole-wheat toast and a large cup of coffee."

"And for you, Mark?" Mr. Hubbard stares at Mark.

"I will have the same, thanks," Mark responds without making eye contact.

"What is wrong with you?" whispers Bev after Mr. Hubbard leaves.

"Nothing is wrong with me," Mark huffs back and crosses his arms.

"Clearly there is something bothering you. From when you woke up until now, you have been obnoxious and rude."

He stares at her, then continues gazing outside at the palm trees and blue water.

"Fine." Bev folds her arms.

When their breakfast arrives, the first ingredient they smell is the rich crispy bacon bits. They cut a portion and the melted mozzarella cheese oozes out of the fluffy omelet. Every bite is better than the last. They eat in silence, and Bev looks up at Mark every so often but he ignores her. When he is done, he rises without saying a word.

"Where are you going?" Bev asks, not amused.

"For a walk, I need to think."

"About what?" Bev asks, stands up to follow him, leaving a half-eaten omelet. She looks back at the delicious meal unsure of what she must do, but goes after him instead.

Mark stops at the dining hall veranda, turns to face her, and whispers, "Can't you feel it? There is something off with that man. The way he speaks to us, the way he speaks to you. You think I didn't see you blush yesterday but I did. And it's this place. And the food. I mean who makes food like that, it's our favorites – how did he even know?" Mark struggles to find the right words. "There is something going on with this place. I don't know what it is, but I don't' like it. I want to leave."

"The food tastes fine to me and what's wrong with him offering us our favorites? He probably phoned your aunt to find out," Bev adds as she walks past him. "If we were to leave, where would we go? We don't have jobs. Try to relax while we are here, use the time to figure out what we are going to do at the end of our stay. Maybe spend this morning on your own, I'm going back to the villa," she says as she walks along the path.

Mr. Hubbard comes up behind Mark once she is gone. "Is everything all right?"

"Everything is fine," Mark says without looking at him.

"Indeed. Well, if you need some time apart, we have a games room. There is table tennis, billiards, a book or two, and even board games."

Mark turns to face his host. "Yeah, maybe, where is it?"

"Follow this path," Mr. Hubbard says, pointing to a path that curves around the dining hall, "look for the building labelled Games Room. It's not that far from here."

"Thanks." Mark walks down the steps and follows the path.

———

When Mark disappears behind the building, Mr. Hubbard takes a walk along the beach. He comes up to Bev's villa and sees her sitting on the bench. He goes up the path and calls out to her. She waves back.

"Here you are." He smiles hypnotically at her, stops at the bottom of the steps. "I wanted to ask after breakfast how you are enjoying your stay, and if everything is in order, but when I came out of the kitchen, you had already left?"

For a split second she is lost in his blue eyes again, and she pauses for a moment too long before eventually answering, "The villa is beautiful; everything is just right, thank you. I don't suppose you would know where Mark is?"

"I do," he says, coming up the stairs.

He stands so close she can smell him; a hint of amber wood, not too strong on the nose, just the right amount. She looks at him and quickly looks away, fidgets with a strand of hair.

Mr. Hubbard continues, "I sent him to the games room behind the dining hall."

"Oh, I didn't see the games room when I went for my walk this morning." Bev rubs the bottom of her top between her thumb and index finger. An old habit she is starting again.

At such proximity she can see the color of his eyes are not only blue; there is a sliver of light green in them. Again she realizes she is staring, and blood rushes to her face.

The left side of his mouth curls up.

"Well, let me know if there is anything else I can do for you." His warm hand touches her arm, and he turns around to descend the steps, before snaking between the other buildings where he disappears.

———

In the games room, Mark is playing table tennis against himself and is winning. It's been a while since he played any type of sport; it has taken him at least twenty minutes to get his hand-eye coordination right. It seems to be working and is somewhat relaxing. He hasn't thought about their troubles. Or is it only his troubles? He can't remember who messed up when, but it seems it's always his fault. Losing his job because of his insecurities, losing their house because there is no money. He has apologized and begged for forgiveness; he knows now she would never cheat on him.

Focusing on the white ball, he needs to ensure he places it within the white line; one more point and he wins. As he hits the last ball, the lights in the room flicker, causing him to lose the point.

"Shit!" Mark sighs under his breath, looks around to see if there is anyone in the room with him, but there isn't. The lights flicker again, but he can't see what the cause is. He moves away from the table when darkness floods the room, and the smell of burnt dry leaves fills his nostrils. A rush of blood courses through his veins as he white knuckles the racquet. Hairs on the back of his neck and forearms rise as a whisper brushes his shoulder. He turns to see who is behind him, but it is too dark. The lights flicker on but there is no one else in the room with him. He turns to face the entrance as the door flings open, and the wind howls outside. The palm trees dance left to right as if they are waving at him. Movement to his right catches his eye, but when he looks in that direction, he holds his breath as he sees a large black shape approach him. His feelings of lone-liness and self-doubt fill his mind once more as he gets knocked down to the ground. The thing is pinning him down. Pressure builds up on his chest as he struggles for air while lying on his back. The heat from the dark thing burns his face, as ash falls from it and lands everywhere. He can't dust the ash away as his arms are heavy. Tears well up in his eyes and burn as the ash falls in them. A cool, sharp object slowly traces its way down his arms – first the left, then down the right. He opens his eyes, and he is lying in a bathtub full of blood.

"No!" Mark cries.

He closes his eyes once more. I don't want to be around anymore. All I do is disappoint Bev. She will be so much happier without me around to drag her down.

"Mark! Mark! Wake up."

He knows that voice. Bev, is that you?

He opens his eyes. "Am I dead?"

Bev chuckles. "No, silly, but you are lying on the floor?"

Mark sits up. "What happened?" He rubs the back of his head.

Bev grabs both his hands and pulls him to his feet. "I don't know. I came in and saw you on the floor. You were crying. Are you all right?"

Wiping away his tears, Mark says, "I think so. It was just a dream, as horrid as it was, just a dream."

"What was it about?"

"Nothing." He brushes past her. "I'm fine. Don't worry about it. What time is it anyway?" He uses the back of his hand to swipe beads of sweat off his forehead.

"Almost lunch. Are you sure you are okay?"

"Yes, I am fine. Come on, let's go."

————

They arrive at the dining hall, but the doors are still locked.

"It's almost 1pm. Let's sit here on the steps," Bev says as they sit down. "Do you want to tell me what happened?" She wraps her arms around him, rests her head on his shoulder.

"It's this place. Weird things are starting to happen, and I want to go." He rests his head on hers, his version of hugging her back.

"Okay, let's find out when the next boat leaves the island."

He nods while keeping his head touching hers.

————

For lunch, Mr. Hubbard offers them two choices again. Bev selects the chicken Caesar salad and Mark, bangers and mash.

How does he really know all our favorites? Did he phone Marks' aunt? Bev thinks to herself halfway through her salad. It tastes so good though. The smokey chicken melts in her mouth, the soft creamy cheese and rich Caesar dressing with fresh crunchy greens. Absolutely delectable.

Mark's richly flavored Cumberland sausage complements the fluffy mash, onion gravy and fried onions. Mark devours his meal in half his usual time.

"Mr. Hubbard?" Bev calls out once they are done.

Mr. Hubbard is about to pick up their empty plates but stops and straightens. "Yes, Bev. What can I do for you?"

"Well..." She pauses, looks over at Mark, but he shrugs. As usual, he doesn't offer any help. Her voice quivers when she continues, "...we were wondering whether we have to stay here for the full three months or can we leave today, or when the next boat leaves?"

Mr. Hubbard's icy blues darken as he towers over her, and his usual jovial face contorts. Bev pushes her chair back against the wall, turns her face away from his wrath.

"Absolutely not! That's out of the question, Bev. You signed a contract. Nobody, I repeat, nobody can leave until their three months are up." He pushes his face right up against hers and thumps his hands on the table. He looks in Mark's direction with the same frightening expression. Mark pushes his chair back in case he needs to make a quick exit.

"I don't understand? We can stay here for free but we can't leave? That doesn't make any sense. Can someone else take our places?"

"I am sorry but no. Your uncle listed you as his next of kin, therefore you have to stay here for the duration." His dark eyes pierce theirs.

Mr. Hubbard steadily backs away from them, his crooked form straightening, his eyes changing back to their casual icy blue while his rage slowly subsides.

He gives them his warm, welcoming smile again and asks, "Will that be all?"

No words. Bev and Mark sit quietly in their seats. She manages to shake her head.

"Good." Mr. Hubbard takes the empty dishes from their table and enters the kitchen.

Bev turns to Mark and tilts her head toward the exit; he nods back. They stand up together and leave.

Once outside and far away, Mark bursts out, "What the hell?"

"I know!" Bev catches Mark's gaze.

"That man is intense."

"What are we going to do?"

"Maybe we should try leave on our own."

"How?"

"I don't know. We can search the island for something to use; maybe there is a boat hidden somewhere? Did you see anything on your walk this morning?"

"That's weird, I can't remember much from my walk this morning." Her brows furrow. "I know it's a small island because it only took me an hour and a half to walk around, but I can't remember anything besides that." Bev shivers.

At their villa, Mark grabs his black cap and gives Bev her white floppy sun hat, and they set off on foot in search of anything they can use to help them escape.

———

Mr. Hubbard stands in the doorway, blocking their path.

"You are late!" he scolds them.

Bev and Mark are only five minutes late for dinner.

"Apologies, we lost track of time," Bev says between deep breaths.

He moves to one side and allows them entry then he goes into the kitchen while they sit down at their usual table. The same kind of wine (chilled) they drank last night is already on their table. Mark pours them each a generous glass. Bev downs hers and asks for more.

"Take it easy. Drink water if you are thirsty."

"I can't help it," she replies, still holding her wine glass near the bottle.

Mr. Hubbard appears with their starters.

"Oh, it's the same starters?" Bev asks.

"Yes, the same. These are your favorites, are they not, Bev?" He is back to his formal monotone.

"Yes, yes, it is. Th-th-thank you very much," Bev stutters, her eyes widening as she locks gazes with Mark.

Mr. Hubbard returns to the kitchen.

"Is it just me or does this feel like that movie where the guy has the same day over and over again?" Mark whispers to Bev. "The same food, at the same table with the same grumpy waiter?"

Bev giggles, downs her second glass of wine, then places the empty glass in front of the bottle for Mark to refill.

"Another?"

"What do you think? I am freaking out right now! The least you can do is fill it up for me."

"Just don't finish the bottle. I want another glass as well." He downs his wine, fills her glass and empties the remainder of the contents into his. "And sip slower."

They eat their starters in silence, apart from the odd giggle from Bev between delicious mouthfuls. Moisture gathers in her eyes, which she nervously wipes away with her napkin.

"I don't know what we are going to do," she says. "I remember us getting our hats and about to search for something to help us get off the island, but it happened again. I can't remember anything we may have seen on our walk. Do you remember?"

He shakes his head, no. "There has to be a boat somewhere. The mainland is only an hour's ferry ride away; it has to come here at some time to drop off guests or supplies for the kitchen," Mark says in a hushed tone.

"I don't know if I want to laugh or cry? I need more wine." Bev downs the rest of her wine.

Mr. Hubbard returns to clear their table and sets down another bottle of wine.

"I see the two of you are starting to enjoy yourselves a little. Finally! Go on, have some more wine." He pushes the open bottle toward Mark and goes back to the kitchen.

Mark downs the little that is left in his glass then refills both glasses with the fresh chilled wine, the cool liquid easing their tension and anxiety.

Bev explodes into giggles when she sees Mark's face contort.

"What is so funny?" he asks.

"Your face! Stop making me laugh!"

"I am not pulling my face," Mark shoots back at Bev. Deep wrinkles form between his eyes and he clenches his jaw.

Laughter consumes her as Mark's face becomes animated.

Mark stands up, takes his glass of wine and sits at the table across from her.

"I am going to eat my dinner over here until you stop laughing." Mark pouts.

"Sorry, come back here?" Bev waves at him to join her again.

He shakes his head.

Mr. Hubbard enters with a chicken breast in lemon sauce and vegetables for Bev and the rump steak and vegetables for Mark. He notices their new seating arrangement and gives Mark his food first and while he places Bev's plate in front of her, he whispers in her ear. She can feel his warm breath on her neck and it sends goose bumps throughout her body, his soothing voice hypnotizing.

Mark watches.

"What did he want?" he demands when Mr. Hubbard returns to the kitchen.

"He told me a silly joke about an old couple who fight. I laughed cause it sounds like us." She downs her fourth glass then pours another.

———

The sensual smell of the steak catches Mark's attention, and he begins to eat, all the while watching her. Her soft cheeks pink, her lips red, he wonders whether it's from the wine or the man's whisper. It reminds him of that dinner they had with his manager before he was fired. Bev got on so well with him – she laughed at his jokes, he would touch her arm every so often; all Mark could do was watch. When dinner was over and they left, they had such a fight where he accused her of cheating. It was all in his head then; could it all be in his head now?

Was it just a joke? Why doesn't she tell me what he said if it was so silly, he keeps thinking over and over again. He keeps his eyes on her, her cheeks still pink. Is he overreacting or is it Mr. Hubbard?

———

Bev takes her time eating; she savors the different tastes of the vegetables, the succulent chicken breast in the salty lemon sauce, the smooth wine complementing her meal. Every bite is more delicious than the last.

She finishes her fifth and fills the glass again.

"Don't you think you have had enough?" Mark asks as he watches her.

"Don't start with me. If I want another glass I will have another glass."

"I can't take this anymore; one moment you want to get off the island, the next you are enjoying his whispers and drinking all the wine."

"I have kept quiet for a while, Mark. I have been there for you during your ups and downs, even when you accused me of the things you thought I did. Not once did I tell you where to get off. Perhaps I should do that now. I am tired and not in the mood for another one of your episodes."

"I am going back to the villa." Hurt, he stands abruptly and leaves.

Mr. Hubbard enters with the desserts and a coffee for Bev, places the items in front of her.

"Has he left you to finish your meal all on your own, my dear?" he asks as he sets the empty plate on the table next to them and sits across from her.

"He was tired."

Mr. Hubbard smiles, peers out the window toward the beach, toward the one palm tree, then stands up and lifts Bev to her feet.

"Dance with me, my dear?"

"Me? Dance? I cannot dance." Bev rocks ever so slightly backward and forward.

"Don't worry, my dear, I will guide the way."

Mr. Hubbard snaps his fingers and a soft melody begins

to play. He pulls Bev closer toward him, her body firmly against his, and guides her as they dance to the music. He kisses her neck gently, sending shock waves throughout her body.

———

Mark stands behind one of the palm trees and sees them dance, sees Mr. Hubbard kiss her neck, then her cheek. He has seen enough and starts walking back to their villa. He cannot fathom what is happening. One moment they were planning their escape, the next she is in that man's arms allowing him to kiss her in the places Mark used to. Is this payback from that one time he screwed up? But this was years ago, and he apologized for his terrible mistake. He was sorry then and he was sorry a couple of months ago when he accused her. He always seems to be doing something wrong then apologizes for it. Maybe she would be better off without him. He still loves her, even though she is in that man's arms right now. His mind races with thoughts he doesn't understand, thoughts he doesn't want to admit. These thoughts involving Bev and Mr. Hubbard overcome him and he runs. He reaches the villa and the sharp pain comes back. He goes straight into the bathroom, where he runs a hot bath. His thoughts are still on replay, what he did to her, what he accused her of, how he treated her. He strips off his clothes and climbs in while the water runs. Only now he notices the blade set on the rim of the bath. Those same thoughts intensify, replaying over and over again, and tears wet his cheeks. Without thinking, he grabs the blade and slices deep cuts into the inside of each arm – wrist to elbow.

Blood flows.

The blade falls out his hand and his arms fall into the

water, turning it crimson. He closes his eyes and falls into darkness.

———

Mark gasps for air as the water fills his lungs, and he sits up and inhales deeply. Somehow he managed to switch off the running water and fall asleep inside the tub. He looks at his arms and heaves a sigh of relief when he sees there are no cuts.

Was it all a dream?

Feeling weak and dizzy, he manages to pull himself up using the railing that's mounted onto the wall and climbs out of the bath. He grabs his robe from the floor and slips it on. Then he opens the bathroom door only to have red-hot air greet him. In the doorway is Mr. Hubbard, or someone who resembles him.

"Mr. Mark McAdams, I have been waiting very patiently for you." The dark figure gloats.

"You have?" A sudden coldness hits him in his core.

"Yes, of course. I only choose the weak, Mark, and you are certainly weak." The dark figure's face changes into a sinister creature that belongs to the night.

Still holding onto the handle to keep his balance, Mark can only stare at the figure in disbelief, trying to piece together what just happened and why. The dark figure doesn't wait for Mark to respond and lifts its arms to reveal large black wings which engulf Mark, pulling him closer toward the darkness and into the red-hot air until they disappear.

———

Bev rests her head on Mr. Hubbard's shoulder while they slow dance. The last time she danced like this was with Mark; she knows she should stop and run after him, but this feels oddly comforting, and she can't pull herself away from him.

"It's time, Bev."

Bev lifts her head to look at the blurry figure holding her. "Huh?"

"You can go back to your villa now." Mr. Hubbard takes her by her hand and they walk outside. She snakes behind him.

When they reach her villa, he opens the door for her and leads her into the bedroom.

"Here, let me help you."

Bev sways left and right, and Mr. Hubbard steadies her then helps her onto the bed. He removes her shoes and covers her with a spare blanket from the cupboard.

He steals a kiss from her and leaves.

———

Her thumping head wakes her, and she smacks her lips together - cotton mouth.

Ugh, again I don't listen, I must not drink so much.

She turns over slowly to face the edge of the bed and pushes herself up. On her bedside table is a note, it reads: 'Drink these' next to two pain tablets and a bottle of water.

How considerate, she thinks as she does what the note says.

She gets out of bed and starts calling Mark's name. When he doesn't respond, she starts looking for him in the spare bedroom, the living area, but he is nowhere to be found. Strange, he has to be somewhere. She heads for the bathroom, pushes the door open slowly as she calls his name. The room has a chill to it and she can see her own breath when she exhales. Still wearing her dinner dress, she hugs her shoulders and walks in. Mark is asleep in the bath, and when she studies his face there is no breath from his mouth. She looks from his face to the dark ruby water, and it takes a few seconds to realize that it's blood. Tears stream down her face and she falls onto her knees. Without thinking she sticks her hands in the water and brings up his right arm to feel for his pulse. She looks away from his sliced arm and darts for the toilet to throw up.

"No!" Her cries echo in the bowl. She gets up and goes to the basin, washes tears away and rinses out her mouth.

She goes to the phone and dials the internal emergency number.

"Hello?" utters a croaky voice from the other side.

"I need help. Please can you send someone. It's urgent!"

"Yes, Mrs. McAdams. Mr. Hubbard will be there shortly."

Bev throws down the phone and sinks into the couch. She knows he has been depressed, but not to this extent. Where did it all go so wrong? She starts biting her nails again, another old habit, and pulls her knees up to her chest and starts to rock.

———

Bev looks up when Mr. Hubbard appears at the doorway.

"Bev? Are you all right?" he asks as he enters, sits beside her and places his arm around her.

"It's not me, it's Mark. He is in the bathtub," she cries through puffy eyes.

He goes to the bathroom where he finds Mark then he

comes back to the living area where Bev has started rocking again.

"It's going to be all right. I will ensure his body is well taken care of. Why don't you go for a walk, perhaps get something to eat or drink?" He grabs her by her hands, gently pulls her to her feet then walks her to the doorway.

"I will join you when I am done."

Hugging her arms, Bev walks slowly up the path to the dining hall where she sits at their usual table. She looks around and realizes there is nobody to bring her breakfast. Bev stands then goes through to the kitchen's double doors to see if she can find something to eat or at the very least a coffee machine.

"Hallo?" she calls out into the large, vacant kitchen. She runs her fingers across the nearest metal table and a thick layer of dust sticks to her skin. She cleans her hand on her dress. On the floor near the walk-in fridge, are a few open boxes with canned food inside, as well as on the greasy floor. She sees a coffee machine on the opposite side of the kitchen and switches it on, starts rummaging through the cupboards for a mug, but they are all empty. There are no dishes in the sink. No pots and pans. No plates. She stands still, places her hands on her hips and scans the kitchen thoroughly, everything coming into focus. She remembers the boxes and goes to the first one and peeks inside. Bev picks up the nearest opened can labelled "Escargot". She lifts the lid and finds maggots crawling inside. She drops the can of food on the dirty floor then begins swiping the maggots off her hands, starts jumping up and down to get them off.

In the next box she finds more tins of food – prawn cocktail, tinned chicken breast, powdered eggs – all the tins are open and full of wriggling maggots, cockroaches and flies. Bev throws up near the boxes, just missing her feet. It is more spit and bile than anything else. They ate this food, it tasted so delicious, delectable and exquisite, at every meal-time. How can Mr. Hubbard give them food that comes from these open tins with maggots and insects crawling inside? Realizing the horror, she runs frantically out the kitchen through the double doors and straight into Mr. Hubbard. He barely moves from the impact whereas she falls backward, hitting the floor coccyx first. She grimaces.

"Mrs. McAdams, where are you rushing off to?" He snickers, reaches for her hand to pull her up, but she is quicker and shuffles backward on her bum toward the swinging double doors. She leans on the nearest chairs to help her get back onto her feet.

"Well, well, well Bev. Quite the feisty one, aren't you?" He takes a step closer.

"I saw the kitchen!" she cries, her body shaking. "You have been feeding us rotten tinned food. What is wrong with you?"

"Ah, you saw that." He grins, revealing his real teeth, filed neatly into killer points.

Bev's eyes grow larger. "Your teeth! What happened to your teeth?" She wipes away a tear.

"Well, Bev, I am called many things but nice isn't one of them."

"What do you want from me?" she asks as she wipes away another tear while fighting the urge to cry again.

"Just your soul!"

"Just my soul?" She takes another step backward until she hits the wall.

"Yes, Bev. Your soul." He moves in closer. "I feed off souls. The more I consume, the stronger I become."

Mr. Hubbard grows larger, darker and his face meaner,

his eyes shift into shiny silver slits. Large dark wings expand from behind him, and he stretches his shoulders out in a circular motion, revealing his true form.

"Ah, this is so much better." His neck cracks from the stretching. "You see, my dear, I collect and feed off souls of those lost in-between Heaven and Hell. What perfect opportunity but here on my island?"

"I haven't killed myself yet. You can't come after me."

"Indeed, but you can't leave either, and I am very patient."

He grins, his teeth becoming sharper and shinier; he flicks his tongue out like a snake. "You see, there is a reason I ask tenants to sign in blood. You sign – you stay. And I will do whatever it takes to push you over the edge while you are on my island and in my villa. The best part is, there is nobody around to help you." His wicked laughter pierces her ears.

"And my uncle."

"Ah yes, your uncle, Timothy Williams. At first he was very hesitant to sign. I never met anyone so afraid of a little pin prick and to sign with his own blood. But envy is such a wonderful sin. Who could refuse an amazing offer; to stay in one of my luxury villas for three months – rent free. I enticed him to come do some research on the island's indigenous animals and plants, but the funny part is there aren't any," he roars.

Bev's hands are clammy against the wall, her heart beating inside her ears. It has only been a few days since Mr. Hubbard pulled a blade from thin air, waved it in front of them and then squeezed their fingers for drops of blood as it oozed into thin glass tubes. Slipped them into a golden quill pen for each of them and they signed on the golden line. Why didn't that raise any alarms with them then? And, why is she only remembering this now?

"Listing a next of kin on a lease agreement is standard practice, so your uncle didn't think twice to add you. His only living relative. He was easy; it only took three days for him to hang himself. But your husband was a record for me, two days." One side of his mouth curls up, his eyes taunting her.

Bev pushes herself from the wall and punches his abdomen. Her hands crunch beneath his ironclad stomach, and she cries in pain. He brings his right hand down, slaps her away like a fly, and she falls across a table, crashes to the floor again.

Staring up at the ceiling, cradling her sore hands, she understands it all now. Why Mark slit his wrists, why he left her alone, why there aren't any other visitors on the island. It's the island's allure. The delicious food, the warm sun on their bodies, the strange atmosphere in the villa, the forget-fulness – all messing with their heads. And, even Mr. Hubbard – the devil in a beautiful body, tempting her.

Still lying on her back and focused on the ceiling, she can hear the monster rambling on, but Bev doesn't listen to what he is saying. Her mind is racing with thoughts on how she can get away. He is too powerful for her to fight, and can kill her instantly if he wants to. Is there a way she can get out? Is there something else she can do? Is there a way she can change the contract? What would she change if she could? Perhaps change the next of kin? If she can change it, whose name would she change it to, and will it even make a difference? There is always a way to get out of a contract. Always. But how? Her friend Lacy is a lawyer and a good one. What would she do?

Bev sits up and sees him perched on the table she

crashed over, peering at her like a bird on a branch. "Before you take me, I want to make one small change to the next of kin on my contract. I am begging for your compassion."

Curious about her request – no one has ever asked this of him in their final hours – all they do is beg and cry, he says, "Okay, I will allow it." He hops off the table, turns around and heads for the door. "Come on, let's go make the change."

She stands up slowly, rubs the parts that ache, and follows the monster version of Mr. Hubbard into his office. He searches for her contract in his filing cabinet and pulls it out then gives her the same golden quill pen with which she signed.

"Cross out the name you have written and make the changes you desire and initial next to it, just like you would any other contract."

"I can choose anybody's name, correct?"

"Yes, my dear, you can put anyone's name there." He certainly is interested in whose name she will write now that she knows what's in store for them.

She wants to put the bully's name from seventh grade out of revenge. She hovers the pen over the contract, then crosses out Natalie Eagle, Mark's aunt.

Mr. Hubbard sits down. "The only stipulation is it has to be someone you know, not a random name, and I will know if you are lying."

Bev pauses, asks, "Are there any other conditions?"

"Nope. Just that you must know them."

"I don't suppose you would share with me if there are any exit clauses?"

"There are but no, I won't tell you." He laughs so hard his body shakes.

She has nothing to lose. Mark is already dead; if she

writes his name, maybe the contract will cancel itself out. With nothing to lose, she writes: Mark McAdams and initials next to the change.

Mr. Hubbard slams his fists down so hard onto his desk the bobble heads fall over, a pope drops to the floor, and he screams, "No!"

Bev freezes, places the gold quill down gently on the desk, keeps her eyes on the monster.

A second after Mr. Hubbard's yell, a tiny flame begins to burn at the corner of her contract. Bev's eyes grow larger while Mr. Hubbard's anger increases.

"No! This has never happened before!" He slaps his desk again and lifts his hand toward the contract.

Bev turns her attention away from Mr. Hubbard and focuses on the piece of paper that caged her on the island and took Mark away from her.

The contract bursts into flames; it burns bright yellow and red with a hint of silvery black. Within a few seconds it disintegrates into ashes, a light wind starts to blow and the ashes fly up and away.

Mr. Hubbard just stands there, stares at Bev, not quite believing someone like her, a housewife, a nobody, managed to cancel his contract.

"Well!" Mr. Hubbard grunts. "It would seem you found one of the exit clauses. Well done, Bev. I guess you are free to go."

Bev smiles, breathes a sigh of relief, and slowly steps backward, away from Mr. Hubbard and toward the door.

"I can go? I can leave and you won't try to stop me or bring me back here?"

"No, I can't stop you. You are free to leave. A boat will be waiting for you when you are ready."

Bev smiles. Mr. Hubbard raises an eyebrow and shoos

her away like a pesky pigeon he doesn't want defecating on his floor.

Bev turns around and darts out his office, sprints all the way to the villa to pack her bags. With a heavy heart, she can't bear to pack Mark's belongings, except for a shirt in which he slept. She lifts it and smells him, weeps for him. They had their issues – which couple doesn't? He did things she didn't like, but she loved him. She misses him. She tucks the shirt into her bag then runs to where the boat dropped them off on that first day.

———

Back in her hometown, Bev stays with her best friend until she gets back on her feet. Mark's life insurance is finalizing the payment upon hearing about his untimely death, and they promise the money will be in her account by the end of the week.

"You have mail, Bev. It's a postcard." Lacy says, entering the house.

"A postcard, from whom?"

Lacy walks over to Bev and hands it to her. "Dunno, found it in the box with your name on."

Bev takes it from her. "Would you like to escape your boring life? Come on over, we have a luxurious villa waiting for you on our island."

Without thinking twice, Bev tears it up and throws it in the dustbin.

Main Course: The Island

Lillian Covington - Ledger Entries

20 May 1866

I befriended a Captain of an old ship who has agreed to take me there. We plan to set sail this afternoon. It is only a four-man crew including the Captain, but he has delicately informed me that he only requires three hands on deck and that they are the best at what they do. I certainly hope so. I have waited fifteen years for this. It cannot fail based on any inadequacies. When I show my son the discovery, he will forgive me. He is studying to become a doctor. His father would be so proud if he were around. I am.

26 May 1866

Captain has assured me we will arrive in the next day or two. I wish he would stop drinking. Last night he didn't anticipate the storm hitting us so hard, there were large waves crashing over us, I was sure we were going to sink. I stayed in my quarters all evening, tied the cupboards' door handles together to stop them from opening and closing as the ship seesawed. I wasn't feeling well and had to drink one of my potent tonics to calm my nerves.

31 May 1866

It's in my line of sight. Captain and his crew thought I lost my mind when I shed tears at the sight of land surrounded by dark wild water. I am so happy to finally see it. Captain circled the Island before he lay anchor. From what I can see, the land is the shape of a very large 'C'. The top curve of the 'C' has high mountainous rocks which no one in their right mind would climb nor can a ship anchor nearby with all the rocks protruding underneath the dark wild water. At the opening of the 'C' is a beautiful beach surrounded by tall palm trees. It is one of the most magnificent landscapes I have ever laid eyes on. Captain agreed that the best place to anchor is at the opening, but cautioned me against leaving the ship today as it is already too dark. The land requires scouting and he and his first mate have agreed to go with me at first light.

1 June 1866

I am too excited to sleep. I couldn't eat breakfast. Butterflies flap their wings inside my stomach. Ecstatic to know that after all these years of searching from one corner of the earth to the other, I have finally found the land. One clue leading me to ten more clues, then fifteen. I sometimes thought it was a hoax. That Frank Covington Sr had sent me on a wild goose chase. I have asked the Captain's third mate to hold onto my diary, all the maps and papers for safe keeping and to send to my son should I not return. My heart wants to beat out of my chest. I cant wait to set foot on the island.

———

Lillian jumps out of the small raft, landing feet first on the soft warm beach sand. She drops her shoes, falls to her knees and picks up a fist full of golden sand. She spreads her fingers to let the sand drizzle through. To her left, Captain jumps out the raft, trips and lands belly first while his first mate pulls the boat to shore and safe keeping for their return. She giggles then stops when he looks up at her, his face red, scrunched up. She bites her lip, sees his first mate giggle and look away too.

"Let me help you up, Captain," she says as she stands up, holds out her hand for him.

"I don't need your help." He grunts as he uses his fists to push up his upper body, and he leans back onto his haunches. Captain stands up and dusts the sand off his clothing and feet, pulls his boots on.

"Ready?" he says while bowing and extending his left arm, allowing Lillian to walk first.

She chuckles as she puts on her shoes then walks ahead of him. Once she is in front, her smile broadens and her shoulders relax with the knowledge that she has finally made it to the island. The beach is surrounded by rows and rows of palm trees and behind them are high rocks with a steep cliff to their right – nearly impossible to climb. To the far left is a gap not visible from the boat, the only section on the beach that doesn't have any rocks. Instead, there are bushes, palm trees and beautiful yellow flowers.

"This seems to be the only way onto the island." She turns to speak to the captain, pointing to the opening. He doesn't answer her.

At the entrance, Captain pipes up, "My turn to lead the

way, Lillian. We don't know what's out there. Follow closely behind me. James will bring up the rear."

"Yes, Captain." Lillian stops and waits for Captain to pass her and take the lead. She looks back at James, who tips his hat at her.

Once through the opening, Lillian feels tiny pin pricks throughout her body. She looks at Captain and James, and they feel the pin pricks too. All three are rubbing their arms, neck and legs.

"What is that?" Lillian asks. She goes back out from where they first came and the tiny pin pricks intensify and disappear as fast as they appeared. "That's strange. It's gone now." She walks back through the entrance and the tiny pin pricks start again. "Very strange. I hope it doesn't continue for our entire journey."

Captain continues to lead them through rough terrain. He takes out his long machete and starts slicing through palm leaves and tree branches. The island is hot and humid, with heat radiating off the rocks. Birds whistle in every direction and the sky is a deep blue. Lillian wipes her brow with her handkerchief and removes her coat to use it as a shield against the leaves and tree branches flying in her direction.

"Can you see anything up ahead, Captain?" she asks.

"All I see are dark rocks up ahead and lots of green leaves and trees. I want to see whether there is a low area where we can climb the rocks for a bird's eye view of the island."

"Good idea!" She exhales, her tongue sticking to the inside of her dry mouth. In her excitement she forgot to pack water. "At least the pin pricks have stopped."

"Lillian, you have been very mysterious as to what is on the island, but could you indicate to us where it is so that we can find our way sooner?" Captain asks, stops to take a break and wipes the back of his neck and forehead with his coat.

"I don't know where it is. Only that it is here somewhere. We need to look everywhere."

"Aha. What is it we are looking for so that we know when we get to it?"

"I will know when we get there."

Captain frowns at her. "The search might go quicker if I have some idea what it is you are looking for."

"It's hard to describe, Captain," is all she can say for now; she doesn't want him to know more just yet.

Thirty minutes later they arrive at the high cliff wall they noted earlier. It consists of the same flat black rock they saw when they circled the island.

"I don't see how we can climb this, Captain? It didn't look this high," Lillian says to him.

The man looks just as tired as she feels. "No idea." He shakes his head. "It will be quicker if we split up." Captain points with his right arm to the right. "You and James go that way, and I will go this way." He points with his left arm in the other direction and starts walking.

"If you can't see a way for us to either climb over this rock or a way around it in ten minutes' time, walk back and wait for me here." He gestures to the spot where they stand. "Don't worry, James will take care of you."

Lillian nods and looks at James, who has now taken the lead. They start walking.

She looks up at the sheer height of the black rocks while

she walks, admiring the beautiful scenery with a scent in the air she tries to figure out, a mixture of sea air, trees and sweet fruit. Her stomach rumbles, she should have eaten breakfast. She turns her head back in search of Captain, but they are already too far apart. All she sees is palm trees to her left and the black rock on her right. She faces forward to see James, trees and more black rocks. Seagulls squawk and she glances up as they fly overhead. After a few steps, she stumbles over her feet and falls. With her palms flat on the ground, she pushes herself up, lifts her head to the left and something in the black rock catches her eye.

"James, look here."

James stops and back tracks to where Lillian fell. "Are you all right, miss?"

"I'm fine, but look, there is a large crack in the rock."

James looks from her to the crack and they both approach what she realizes is an entrance.

"Yes!" Lillian jumps up and down. "This is it, James. Let's go in."

They pass through the narrow aperture, Lillian still dusting sand off her soiled dress; she finds a large tear – it's a small price to pay in comparison with what she hopes they might discover within this dark rock. Her eyes adjust to the low light. Using the walls of the cave to guide her, she meanders inside. Completely engulfed in blackness, she can feel the cool air blowing around her. The refreshing wind against her skin cools the sweat off her face and arms. The fresh air fills her nostrils and lungs, and she inhales deeply.

She stands still, closes her eyes and takes it all in. Her breathing slows.

Slowly in. Slowly out.

When she opens her eyes and focuses on the twilight,

silver light cascades from a hole in the ceiling that reflects off the calm water. She walks slowly, deeper inside the chamber, inching closer to the edge of the water, where she kneels. Lillian cups her hands and scoops water to drink. The invigorating liquid cools her warm mouth and s it slides down her throat, into her stomach. Energized, she wants more. She slips off her shoes, places her coat on top of her shoes and walks into the water. Gradually moving deeper with each step, she submerges and fills her mouth with water which she swallows. Her face and hair wet, Lillian comes up for air then dives again, swimming deeper and for as long as her lungs can manage.

"Lady Lillian?" a familiar voice asks.

She turns toward the opening of the cave, to the two silhouettes. One of the shadows lights something, and there is a bright flame. It is James. He places the flame between rocks and kneels so he can quench his thirst.

Captain exclaims, "What happened?"

She swims closer to them, Captain approaching her, his mouth agape.

"What is it?" she enquires.

"You, Lillian, it's you. You have changed. You look different. You look so much younger." Captain's mouth gapes wider, and he removes his hat and holds it with both hands.

"I feel so good. I haven't felt this wonderful in many years. You should try it," Lillian calls after them, swims to the edge, climbs out of the water and goes to him. With her hand she closes his mouth. He blinks at her, keeps his mouth closed.

"Are my eyes deceiving me? Is it really you?" Captain says, rubbing his eyes.

"This is why we are here. It's for this water, for Pure

Water." She smiles at him. "Come inside. You will feel so much better. The pain in your elbow that you mask will heal."

She takes his hand and leads him to the water. He drops his hat and coat on a rock and removes his boots.

"Oh my! The water is cold," he exclaims.

Lillian lets go of his hand and swims ahead of him.

"I can't swim," he confesses, his cheeks glow.

"You don't have to swim. Walk in as far as you can, quench your thirst and wet your body. You too James?"

James shakes his head. "Only a little, ma'am." He drinks some of the water and sits down, puts his feet in.

Captain nods, pinches his nose closed and goes under the water. Then he enjoys a drink where he is and comes up. He goes underwater again and back up.

Lillian bears witness to the aging process in reverse. Once a bulky, scar-ridden, gray-haired, fifty-something-year-old man, he has transformed into a handsome, twenty-something with smooth skin and light brown hair, who is healthy again.

He comes up again and just stands there, stares at Lillian. She swims closer to Captain, and they lock gazes. They smile at each other. For the first time in years she feels well again, rejuvenated and revitalized. She can only imagine how Captain must feel if this is how it is for her. They return to shore, neither saying a word, apart from a few childish giggles.

Once out the water, Captain says, "I had no idea such a place existed. No wonder you kept this secret all to yourself. Imagine what man can accomplish if in the right hands."

"I didn't want to say anything before, for reasons you now understand. It is wonderful, wouldn't you agree?"

"Indeed, but how did you know about this place?"

She opens her mouth to answer his question, but the sting in her neck causes her vision to blur and she falls to the ground. Captain crashes down beside her. With all his strength he grabs her hand for comfort.

———

A wild man stands above Captain, holds a sharp spear to his neck and asks, "What should we do with them?"

Captain lies unconscious beside Lillian and James, on a bed made from reeds. Lillian opens her eyes just enough to be able to see who is surrounding them without them knowing she is awake.

"Not sure?" says someone from the back.

Another replies, "This woman looks vaguely familiar."

"I know her!" shouts a man, who is running toward the group, toward her.

"I know her," he repeats when he reaches them, near her.

"Well? Who is she?" the same man asks.

"She is my wife."

With those four words, Lillian opens her eyes completely. She can no longer pretend to be unconscious in the hope that the island inhabitants will leave them alone. Her dead husband's voice has forced her to move. She sits up and stares at him. The man she married thirty years ago, who is supposed to be dead, is standing in front of her. Their youthful eyes lock in recognition. He smiles at her. With all her might she kicks him in the shins.

"Argh," he cries. "What did you do that for?"

"For leaving me," she says. "For leaving us. We thought you were dead."

"You found my ledger, didn't you?"

She nods.

"Did you find my letter explaining everything?"

Another nod.

"It was all in there, Lillian. The map, stating the last place I was on my way to. You were supposed to come find me."

"You should have taken us with you," she replies, frowning.

His face softens at her expression and he kneels, one knee on the ground, reaching for her hands.

"I am sorry, my dear. I thought you understood my clues. I couldn't just say where I was going and what I was looking for. What if my ledger ended up in the wrong hands? This place would be ruined."

She allows him to kisses her hand.

Keeping her hands in his, he pulls her up to her feet. She looks out onto the blue sea, the ship they arrived on is no longer in the place where they anchored it, where they left it before coming to shore.

"Where is Junior?"

"In England, studying to become a doctor."

"How old can you be to study to become a doctor? Junior is only ten?" he exclaims.

"Our son isn't ten, Frank. He is almost twenty-eight."

"Well I'll be darned. Twenty-eight already, I stopped counting the days long ago. I was hoping you would have brought him with on your trip." He smiles at her, brushes a strand of hair out of her face. "Why did you take so long to get here?"

"Your clues were not very clear, my dear. I have been searching for this place all on my own while Junior stayed with Martha."

"Martha!"

"My sister did a fine job taking care of him."

Lillian's frustration is pushing her to her limits, and she places her hands on her hips. All the expeditions she went on searching for the island were difficult, and she couldn't go on them with a ten-year-old by her side. She had to leave him where he would be safe.

"We can always go back and fetch him?" she adds.

"My darling, unfortunately not. Once you are here you can never leave. You can never go back."

The wild man confirms this by lifting his spear toward her face. Lillian backtracks, holding her hands in the air in surrender.

"What about our son, Frank?" she cries, searching Frank's face for benevolence.

She has already missed out on her son's early years; she can't miss his future too. This discovery means nothing if he can't share it with them. Her chest pains at the thought.

"No one has left this island alive, Lillian. These are the consequences of eternal youth. That tingling feeling you felt when you first entered the island, that slows down time for us and speeds up time outside. So, who knows what year it is out there, in any case. It doesn't matter after a while. I am sorry. There was no way of knowing and no way to tell you."

Lillian cannot believe what her husband is saying. If only she had known. She would have brought Junior with. Now he has lost both his parents. Frank embraces Lillian, and she buries her face in his chest. At least she has her husband back; they can live their days together, forever.

There is a commotion up ahead which pulls them apart. Lillian holds onto Frank's hand as they walk to where the crowd has gathered. Approaching up the rocky steps is a man no one knows; when he gets closer to them, Lillian's face lights up. He is a little bit older, at least five or six years, but it is he. She knows those green eyes anywhere.

"Junior!"

Dessert: Deadly Nightshade

Olivia's tired eyes strain to focus on the figure in front of her. She nods and accepts the vial in her wrinkly, sun-kissed hand, gripping the one thing that can save her. The vial is easy enough to open and she drinks every drop. The sweet honey-berry mixture with a bitter aftertaste relaxes her trembling mind. Visions of her late husband flash before her as she reaches out to grab his hand – grabs air instead. Tears wet her cheeks, but they aren't tears of sadness; they are tears of joy. Olivia will soon be with her Martin, and her parents who are long gone.

Her last ten minutes are blissful, her last second, peaceful.

Her death, compassionate.

———

Harriet is always on time. This week at Penny-Lane she clocks in at six a.m. then clocks out six p.m. At 6:10 a.m, Harriet finishes her second cup of coffee and enters room

600 where Moira Myers is still asleep. Moira's teeth are floating in the glass on the bedside table, and Harriet's coffee rises at the back of her throat. Teeth. Dentures in a solution next to an old sleeping goat. She opens the curtains and the window for some fresh air; the air-con on their floor still isn't working. She makes a mental note to tell the electrician. Across the hall is room 602, Oliver Martinez. He is already awake and walking at a snail's pace toward the bathroom.

"Oliver, let me help you," cries Harriet as she enters his room, supports him under his arms and guides him.

"Morning Nurse Harriet. When I am done here can I have my sponge bath?" he asks cheekily, giving Harriet a sly smirk.

"I'm afraid not. Today you need to have a proper shower," she replies with her nose pointed at the ceiling.

When they reach the bathroom, she pulls down his pajama bottoms and helps him onto the toilet.

"Look over there, Oliver. We installed a brand new seat for you to sit on while you shower. Are you going to try it out for us today? Maybe after you're done here?"

"Whatever you say," he responds. "You know what? Maybe just help me back to my bed; I don't think I am up for a shower so early anyway. Maybe after breakfast?"

"Sure, Oliver. After breakfast it is then."

―――――

Harriet knows he won't shower after breakfast; she can see the pain in his gray eyes. The short walk from his bed to the bathroom has already taken its toll. He finishes his business on the toilet and she helps him back into bed. She goes to his medical chart that sits at the foot of his bed and writes a note for Michael to possibly recommend a catheter for him.

The next room she enters is 604, which is across the corridor again. Whoever designed the floor labeled each room across from one another instead of in a row.

"Morning, Molly," Harriet says as she enters her room.

"Morning Nurse Harriet. How are our little darling girls doing today?"

"Well, the little one is off to school with the big one today, and they are both excited."

"Aah, I remember the days when my babies were off to school. As you know back then schools were very different. These days the kids have guns, knives and need to walk through metal detectors to get into school."

Harriet giggles at the old lady. "Luckily for now, mine are only in grade school. I will worry about the guns and knives when they get older."

She opens Molly's curtains then helps her sit up. Harriet fluffs her pillows for her.

"Thank you, dear. Can you help me find the remote before you leave?" Molly says while looking for the lost item. "Aah."

"Hold on, let me help you lie back down. Your remote is here where you left it, next to your bed." Harriet hands her the remote.

"Tommy will be in shortly to give you your breakfast."

"Just as long as it's not eggs again. I almost spat out my teeth yesterday."

Harriet laughs; here goes another denture story. "I will let you know if it's eggs, but I doubt it. On Fridays the chefs like to surprise this floor with something a little tastier."

Harriet moves across the corridor to the next room, 604.

"Morning, Mike. Lovely day today. Can I open your curtains a bit?"

"Argh!" Mike Fields cries from under the covers.

"Not having a good one today, are you?" She keeps his curtains closed and goes to his bedside. "How are your pain levels today?"

"Terrible, just terrible, Nurse Harriet."

"Okay, remember you can only have your pain meds after you have eaten. I will ask Tommy to bring your breakfast first. Will that do for you?"

"Okay," the small man cries from the safety of his bed.

She leaves Mike's room and stops just outside his door. On the outside of each door is a see-through holder where the nurses or doctors can place color cards to highlight a certain need. She takes out the red (food first) and black (pain) cards and slots them in next to each other.

The next room is 608, Olivia Larson. Harriet enters and goes straight toward the curtains and opens them. Olivia loves the morning breeze, so she leaves the window ajar.

"Morning, Olivia, it's such a beautiful morning," Harriet greets her as she normally does. When Olivia doesn't respond, Harriet turns toward the bed, comes in a little closer and sees Olivia's lifeless body. She moves a strand of white hair out of Olivia's face and closes her eyes. Harriet whispers, "Rest in peace, precious lady."

Once outside the room, Harriet takes out a white (deceased) card, places it in the see-through holder, and goes to the nurses' station near the elevator to report her death.

———

The elevator doors open and Tommy emerges, pushing the

food trolley. He stops at the nurses' station to greet Nurse Harriet, tucks some of his loose red hair behind his ears.

"Morning N-Nurse Harriet. How are you today?"

"Morning, Tommy, as good as expected. How are you?" Before he can reply, she continues, "Can you tell me, are our patients eating eggs for breakfast?"

"I am g-good, thanks. N-Nope, it's French toast with honey and cinnamon."

"Good. Mrs. Sims hates the eggs. Tommy, before you go anywhere, Mr. Fields in room 606 is in pain, can you see to it that he gets his breakfast first so that I can give him his pain medication?"

"Okay, I will go now." Tommy looks up and sees the two cards in the see-through holder on Mr. Fields's door frame, the black and the red, and heads in that direction. He looks one door across the corridor and sees the white card.

"She die? Mrs. Larson?"

"Yes, Tommy. She passed away last night."

"I liked her. She was always kind to me."

"We all did, Tommy. Now could you go to Mr. Fields quickly?"

"Yes, going there now." Tommy pushes his trolley past the other doors and heads straight to room 606.

Harriet sits down on the chair and picks up the phone.

———

Dr. Michael Alastair swallows hard. No matter how many times he hears this about one of his patients, it saddens him. He composes himself and puts down the phone then walks to the back door.

"That was Harriet. Olivia Larson died last night," he

calls out to his wife from the doorway, watching her as she works in her garden.

"Peacefully, I hope?" Vanessa asks without looking up. She pulls out a weed and throws it to the side. Her wavy brown locks flow in the breeze.

"Always, my dear."

She looks up, her brown eyes meeting his. He gives her a comforting smile.

"Good," Vanessa replies then clips a few berries from her Atropa belladonna plant and places them neatly in her basket.

"Are you making more?" Michael walks down the three steps toward her while he sips his lukewarm coffee.

"Yes, I gave you the last one yesterday." Vanessa stands up, pulls off her gloves, then places them in her basket alongside the berries, stems and leaves of the deadly nightshade. She turns around and approaches Michael, takes his cup out of his hands and finishes his coffee.

"Are you ready for your own cup?" He smirks at her, takes back his cup.

"Yes, I think so." She smiles then follows him back inside the house. "Did anyone see?"

"No. When Tanya needed the bathroom I told her I would do my rounds until she got back."

"You know, you can't keep doing that. One day someone is going to suspect." Vanessa places her basket on the kitchen table, washes her hands then turns to face Michael.

"Nobody knows anything." Michael holds his wife's face and plants a delicate kiss on her forehead.

"Until one day when someone sees you." She folds her arms to put some distance between them.

There is concern in her eyes; he unhooks her arms and wraps them around his waist.

"Okay, here's the deal. I won't do it when I am the only one around. I will wait until the nurse is there and do it in front of them." He chuckles at the thought.

Vanessa un-wraps her arms and strikes his chest with her fists.

"Okay, I am sorry. Poor joke." He grabs her for another embrace. "I will be more careful, I promise. I will ask them to wait until after I leave, okay?" He looks into her rich chocolate eyes and kisses her full lips.

"Okay," she responds, hugs him back and gives him another kiss before letting go.

"How long has Harriet worked with you?"

"I think she is going on eight years already. The other two are still new by comparison," he responds then goes to the counter where the coffee percolates, for a refill. He stops mid-task and asks her, "You?"

She nods yes, and he takes a cup out the cupboard and pours hers first and then for himself.

"It's a long time to work in such a place, surrounded by so much death."

"I'm going on thirteen years already. What does that say about me?"

"You're different; you don't work twelve-hour shifts. Besides, you are not the one who finds them."

"True." He looks down, remembers all his patients who have passed away throughout the years – most of them due to natural causes.

"There is a high staff turnover, as you can imagine. I think Harriet is at that age where she is done moving from job to job and will retire here."

"What are your plans today my dear?" He asks changing the subject.

"Me, you ask?" she replies, her eyelashes fluttering. "Thought you would never ask. I was thinking of finishing the painting Finn is bugging me for." She rolls her eyes. "The person who bought it, is leaving for Europe soon and wants to take it with him. So I have a few days left before Finn comes and fetches it from me. Then, as you can see, I am going to make more nightshade."

"You should tell Finn not to sell your pieces until you have actually finished them."

"They usually buy what's hanging in the gallery, but Finn said the buyer commissioned the piece."

"At least they are selling again." He smiles at her and gives her another kiss. "I need to go, before Harriet phones again." Michael places his empty cup in the basin, gives his wife a last kiss and heads for the front door. "See you around seven tonight?"

"Yes, see you at seven."

"Before I forget. The nightshade took a bit long, unless that was what you were aiming for?" Michael stops at the front door, one hand pushing the screen door open.

"Why do you ask, did something happen?" Vanessa asks while walking toward him.

"Nothing happened. She mumbled a little more than usual and then she started grasping the air and then..." He can't finish the sentence.

"Okay, it may not have been strong enough. I will adjust the new batch." She pecks his cheek.

"Thanks, love, see you." Michael closes the screen door and heads down toward his car.

"Bye." Vanessa waves at him as he drives away.

———

A loud clank and a bang draws Vanessa's attention to the house next door. An old removal van stops outside the neighbors' house inches away from hitting the fence. She wants to yell at the driver, but stops herself when she sees a young woman climb out to check the distance between the vehicle and the fence. The woman sees Vanessa and waves; Vanessa waves back.

"Morning!" the woman yells. "I'm Jenny Mason, this is my daughter, Gracie." Jenny leans into the van and carries out a petite girl holding onto a brown teddy bear.

Vanessa walks down her front porch steps and along the little path, then stops at the little gate. She watches the young mother approach with the little girl on her hip. The child's hair is unbrushed, and dirt marks one side of her face.

"Hi, I'm Vanessa Alastair. Hi, Gracie."

Gracie hides her face in her mother's bosom.

"How old is she?"

"Almost two."

"Welcome to the neighborhood. Where did you move from?"

"Not sure if you have heard of Jackson Falls. It's a small town up north?"

Vanessa shakes her head.

Jenny kisses Gracie on the top of her head. "Anyway, it was lovely to meet you, but we must go. I still have lots of unpacking to do."

Vanessa smiles. "I guess we will see you around then. Good luck with unpacking."

Vanessa turns and heads back up the path to her stairs.

"Bye," Jenny says and goes back to the van.

Once she's inside, Vanessa locks the screen door, bolts the main door shut, and goes to her study to finish the artwork for Finn.

———

Nurse Harriet continues, "I got in at six this morning, started my rounds at 6:10a.m. And found Mrs. Olivia Larson had passed away sometime during the night or this morning."

Michael nods and scribbles in Olivia's medical file. "Thank you, Harriet. Is there anything else before I send the file to Dr. Orion?"

"No," she answers then looks up from where she is standing and sees the black and red cards across the corridor. "Oh yes, Mike is complaining about pain, and Oliver might need a catheter."

"Sure, I will check in with Mike first."

"Thank you."

Harriet leaves Michael in room 608 then tends to the rest of the patients in Penny-Lane. Michael closes Olivia's medical file and places it on top of her lifeless legs. He can hear the unmistakable clunk of Tommy's trolley and goes to the door.

"Tommy," Michael calls out to him from the doorway.

The young man looks up in Michael's direction.

"Tommy, when you are done, will you take Mrs. Larson downstairs to the morgue?"

"Yes D-Dr. Alastair. I am almost d-done collecting the empty breakfast plates."

"Great, thanks, Tommy. One more thing, I left the medical file on top of her legs. Will you make sure Dr. Orion gets it."

"Yes d-doctor." Tommy nods and continues with his task.

Michael leaves room 608 and goes across the corridor to room 606. Mike Fields is sitting up waiting for him.

"Mike, what can I do for you today?"

"I don't think the pain medication is working, doctor. I am always nauseous, my body still aches, and it feels as though my head wants to explode." Mike rubs his temples with a pained expression.

"Let me take a look."

Michael performs the usual checks, temperature, blood pressure, ears, nose and throat. Then he removes the medical chart from the metal pocket hanging from the foot of Mike's bed, checks which medication he is on, and writes a note for Harriet.

"All right, I have made some adjustments to your dosage. Tell the nurse how you feel throughout the day, and if nothing works, I will consider changing your pain medication. I want you to try these adjustments first before we continue."

Mike nods then sinks back down into his bed and pulls the covers over his shoulders.

Michael places the medical file back in the metal pocket and closes the door when he leaves.

He understands the pain his patients go through; he saw it with his mother and then his sister. They both suffered the aftereffects of double mastectomies, hair land weight loss, and severe pain. The chemotherapy to kill the cancer killed them instead, and his father died of a broken heart. Thinking of his family only leads him to think of Amelia, their only child. He pushes those memories of her to the side, and considers Mike Fields instead, an 81-year-old who lived alone all his life. He doesn't have any children (that he knows of), no brothers or sisters, and his parents died a long time ago. He is an old man suffering from a disease no one cares to cure, and all he can do to help is make him comfortable by offering him pain killers.

When his good friend Dr. Vincent Samuels offered him a position at this wing, a place where terminal patients could be properly cared for during their final days, he had to take it. And, when they are ready to leave, he will make sure they go peacefully and with dignity.

Harriet steps out into the corridor the same time Michael does and greets him, "See you this afternoon."

"Bye, Harriet. I left a note for you in Mike's chart, I don't think there is anything to worry about. Give me a call if he complains again."

"Will do, thanks, doctor."

"Another thing. I don't want to prescribe a catheter for Oliver just yet. I want him to walk as often as he can. I'm concerned his health might deteriorate once we insert it," Michael adds as he and Harriet walk in the same direction.

"Sure, it makes sense."

Michael goes down the two flights of stairs to his consulting rooms.

———

It's 6:20pm and Michael is finishing up with his evening rounds at Penny-Lane before heading home. Simon, the only male nurse at the hospital, relieved Harriet and is standing with Dr. Alastair at Mike's bedside.

"Yes, Dr. Alastair. I feel a bit better."

"It's my pleasure. Get some rest, and give Simon a call if the pain becomes unbearable again."

"Thank you." Mike smiles as he lies back down.

Dr. Alastair pats Mike's leg then they leave his room.

"What was that all about? Harriet didn't mention any changes to me?" Simon asks once they reach the privacy of the nurses' station.

"No, she wouldn't have. I wanted to test something. Mike wasn't feeling well this morning, that he was experiencing more pain than usual. Firstly, his pain meds are already at a high dose, and I didn't want to increase the dosage until I understood how much pain he was in. Sometimes patients just need extra attention. I left a note for Harriet to give him his usual meds and to add a sugar tablet. As you can see, the original dosage is fine, and he is managing okay at the moment. But, will you keep an eye on him for me throughout the evening and the weekend?"

"Sure. Are you coming in on the weekend or should we call you on your cell if we need anything?"

"Give me a call if there is an emergency only. I promised the Mrs. we would do something this weekend." Michael hands Simon Mike's medical folder. "Would you mind putting this back for me?"

"Sure. Have a good weekend, doctor."

"You too, Simon."

Michael is about to leave when he hears a faint voice calling his name. He follows the whimper.

"Dr. Alastair…Dr. Alastair..." the person cries.

It's the patient from room 618, Dr. Herbert Walsh.

"Herbert, are you calling after me?" Michael asks when he enters his room.

"Dr. Alastair," whispers Herbert, "I am ready to dance in the shade of the night."

Michael stands close to his bed and looks him in the eye. "Where did you hear that?"

"Olivia." Herbert whispers, "She explained to me what

it means and what you have done for the others. Please help me too."

"Are you sure?"

Herbert nods.

"Why?"

"I am ninety-two years old, my children and grandchildren are all over the country and busy with their own lives. And, you know what it says on my chart. I can't take the pain anymore, Dr. Alastair. The discomfort. I can't even take a piss without wetting myself. It's like my body isn't even mine." Herbert rubs his eyes. "I am ready, ready to dance in the shade of the night." He winces as he gives Michael half a smile, holds his breath and rubs his abdomen.

Michael moves closer to him, places his hand on the old man's chest and nods.

Loud footsteps outside the door are followed by Simon's voice, "Hey, Doc, you still here?"

"Yes Simon, what's wrong?" He removes his hand from Dr. Walsh's chest then turns to face Simon as he enters.

"Oh, nothing. I saw you come in here and I wondered if there is anything I can assist you with?"

"I am not here, I am going home. I was just checking in with Herbert quickly." Michael turns to the old man. "I will see you first thing on Monday morning." He pats his leg and winks.

Michael says to Simon, "Take care of my patients."

———

Vanessa finishes the last stroke of the painting for Finn. It's one of my best, she thinks to herself as she stands there admiring it. She hears the garage door open, then close.

Michael is home. She will wait for him in her studio. She can hear him open the door that leads from the garage into the kitchen, throw his keys in the key bowl then stomp up the steps.

"Essa, where are you?"

"In here."

Michael enters her studio, slightly out of breath. "How was your day?"

"Good, how was yours?"

Michael pulls Vanessa into his arms and they kiss. Michael embraces her a little longer than usual.

"It was good, and we have another one." He gives her the look, one eyebrow raised, both eyes bigger followed by an intense stare. Not very scientific but they understand the meaning.

Already?" She gives him the look back.

"Yeah. He is at the ripe old age of ninety-two and in bad shape. Vincent only gave him two to three months, and he is already on his fourth. He needs a little nudge," Michael answers her. He studies the painting. "This is beautiful." He starts playing with the paint brushes standing in the jar of thinners on the table.

"The next batch is ready. You can take one on Monday morning."

He takes her in his arms. "Right now all I want is you."

———

Vanessa leaves Michael to rest. It's already after 9pm, and they haven't eaten dinner yet. She goes downstairs to the kitchen to prepare something light, a chicken salad or turkey sandwiches. Vanessa decides on both, which they can share. She sets place mats on the kitchen counter with a plate and fork on each then prepares the two meals and covers the turkey sandwich with a plastic cover while using clear wrap over the salad bowl.

Michael moves about upstairs.

"Hun, are you hungry?" she calls out to him while standing at the foot of the stairs with one hand on the railing. "I rustled up something for us to eat."

She goes back to the kitchen where she takes two wine glasses out of the cupboard, fetches the chilled red wine from the fridge, and sets them neatly on the counter.

"I'm famished," Michael yells from upstairs. "I will be right down."

She opens the bottle of wine, pours them each half a glass then takes a sip from hers and licks her lips. Michael skips downstairs. His mood certainly has shifted. She smiles to herself.

"This looks great," Michael says when he arrives and takes a sip of his wine. "Hmm, this tastes better."

"Come, let's eat. I wasn't sure what you felt like eating, so I thought we could share?"

"You know me too well; this is perfect."

They sit down and Vanessa gives them each half a sandwich while Michael shares the salad between them. They both start with the sandwich.

Wailing in the distance causes Michael to stop chewing and look up. "Is that a child crying?" he asks.

"It could be our new neighbors, a young mother and her little girl."

"About time. That place has been empty for a while."

"The agent must have given her quite a discount."

"Should I go see if she is okay? It sounds like she is in pain."

The crying continues in the background.

"It couldn't hurt? Let me come with you."

Michael goes to the entrance and opens the coat cupboard, picks up his spare medical bag and they walk hand in hand to their new neighbor's house. Vanessa rings the doorbell. The sound of a crying baby becomes louder after the first ring. Through the frosted glass, they see a figure approach the door then open it.

A distraught mother stands in front of them with a crying baby on her hip. Her bloodshot eyes light up when she sees Vanessa.

"Jenny," Vanessa says to the young mother. "This is my husband, Michael. He is a doctor. We heard your daughter's shrill crying and thought he could help?"

"You could hear her cry all the way from your house?" Jenny says looking from their house to them.

"Yes, we could hear her from our house. Would you like me to have a look?" Michael says as he reaches for the screen door.

"Thank you, that's very kind of you. I have never had the pleasure of a house call before. Please excuse the mess. I haven't unpacked everything yet," Jenny says while backing away for Michael and Vanessa to enter.

Jenny pushes a plastic bag onto the floor then places crying Gracie on the only piece of furniture in the lounge – a two-seater couch.

Michael glimpses medicine bottles in the plastic bag Jenny pushes onto the floor and watches how she miss-steps and regains her footing. Her behavior reminds him of his patients when their medication starts to take effect. He gets down onto his knees in front of Gracie, places his medical bag next to him and asks Jenny. "Can you tell me what you think is bothering her?"

"I don't know. She started crying about an hour ago and hasn't stopped."

"And some of her history, anything I might need to know?"

"Ever since she was born she has been sick, in and out of hospital," Jenny answers as she flops down next to her daughter.

"Can you elaborate?" Michael pulls out his stethoscope.

"She was admitted for ear infections, seizures, high fevers and some stomach problems."

"Let me take a look." Michael turns to his young patient. Jenny wants to prop her on her lap, but Michael stops her. "Don't let her sit on your lap. I need her to sit on her own, just for the vitals and then you can take her again."

Jenny gets up to give him space and stands next to Vanessa.

"Hey Gracie," Michael says softly to the little girl, while he warms the stethoscope in his hands. "This here is what I am going to use to listen to your heart. Would you like to listen to my heart first?"

Gracie nods and allows Michael to place the earpiece in her ears and the chest-piece near his heart. Her eyes widen when she hears the doctor's heartbeat, and she giggles.

He takes the earpiece out of her ears and asks, "Can I listen to your heart now?"

Gracie nods.

Michael continues with his routine: temperature, blood pressure, ears, nose and throat. He feels for any tender spots on her stomach, and everything seems fine, apart from inflamed tonsils and swollen glands.

In the plastic bag next to him Michael notes some of the

names on the bottles, all pain killers, all for Grace, and all empty. He closes his medicine bag and decides against giving Jenny one of his samples, instead writing a prescription. He gives Gracie her little brown teddy bear to hold and stands up.

"She has tonsillitis, Jenny. Here is her prescription. You can fill it tomorrow morning. For now you can give her any pain relief you have here at home."

"We do have some left." Jenny bends down to pick up Gracie. "Thank you so much."

"If her fever continues tonight, give her the pain suspension every two to three hours until it breaks, but if it doesn't, call me."

"I will, thank you."

Michael and Vanessa leave the young mother and head back to their house in silence.

———

Saturday morning goodness shines into their bedroom. Michael stretches first and then Vanessa, before she wraps her arms around him.

"Morning," Michael says while yawning then kisses Vanessa's forehead. "Let's go for a boat ride."

"That sounds like a plan. Can we stop at the harbor, get some breakfast and then go for a walk?" Vanessa asks, still holding onto Michael.

"Sure. Did you hear the little girl cry again?"

"No, I didn't, did you?"

"No, but I do think we should pop over before we leave?"

Their house sits on the river bank with ten other houses on Pine Street. Their backyard is the river, and at their front yard is the road and then a forest with high trees – the best of both worlds.

At least three times a month, Michael and Vanessa take their boat out and sail on the river into town. This morning they take it easy, dress in summer clothing, but include a warm jacket for the boat ride. They enjoy a cup of coffee then stroll down the path toward Jenny's house. At her door, Michael knocks three times, and when nobody answers, he knocks three more times.

"Maybe she went to fill your prescription?" Vanessa looks through the window for movement inside the house.

"Maybe," Michael replies. "Come, let's go."

They leave Jenny's house and walk the path back through their garden down to the river. The boat house shelters their mariner sail boat from the elements and doubles as Michael's workstation where he keeps his tools – which he only uses when he absolutely has to. Vanessa climbs into the boat and dusts the seats, throws the cloth under her seat and sits down. Michael loosens the ropes then assumes position at the wheel. They exit the boat house.

The weeping willows on the water's edge greet them as they float past; there are no other sounds except for their boat and the few birds that sit in the trees and call out to one another. Michael wears his boat hat and Vanessa wraps her shawl around her head to keep her hair neat and to stay warm. She lifts her face toward the sun to absorb the rays. Thirty minutes later, they whir in at the small harbor where Michael docks in his usual spot. Old man Luc sees them, approaches their boat then helps them dock.

"Doc, Mrs. Alastair," Luc greets them.

"Morning, Luc," Vanessa and Michael say in unison.

Michael continues, "How is the family doing, Luc? Is your wife feeling better?"

"Much better. She still gets a headache once in a while, but the cough is gone." Luc and Michael shake hands as Michael steps onto the platform. Luc helps Vanessa out of the boat.

"Good," Michael continues, "we're just having breakfast. We should be back soon."

"No problem. See you when you get back."

"Thanks, Luc, see you later."

Michael and Vanessa walk hand in hand down Main Street, toward The Angry Angler. They greet everyone they know and enter the restaurant. They sit near the window, the best view of the town, and enjoy the warm sun on their backs. The owner, Betsy, greets them and brings them menus. Before she leaves, Michael and Vanessa order their hot beverage and breakfast. One of the things Michael and Vanessa love about staying in a small town is that they know almost everybody and receive overwhelming support from the community, who thrive on traditional values. On the downside, a person can't move here if they desire anonymity.

Michael and Vanessa enjoy their breakfast and finish before the morning rush. Once outside in the warm air, they continue their walk along Main Street and head back to the harbor, stopping at various antique shops to admire the old and new.

When they reach the entrance, Dr. Anthony Jeffreys approaches them. "Michael," Anthony says, reaching out to shake Michael's hand. "Hi, Vanessa," he says, with a hug for her.

Vanessa says hi and hugs him back then Michael continues, "Anthony, how are you?"

"Good. I met your neighbor last night?"

Michael and Vanessa look at each other then back at him.

"Which one?" Michael asks.

"Jenny Mason and her daughter Grace. I was on call last night when they came into the ER. It was around 11pm, I think."

"Really, what was wrong?"

"A high fever and tonsillitis."

"I see," Michael says, glances at Vanessa, who is frowning.

Michael continues, "Did she mention that I consulted her daughter around nine last night? I know I am not a pediatrician, but I heard the poor girl crying from our house and had to help."

"That's odd. She never mentioned you treating her daughter, just that she lives next door to you." Anthony's brow furrows. "Anyway, I kept her in the ward for observation and instructed that she be discharged this morning with take-home medication."

Take-home medication. Prescribed medication. A bag full of empty pill bottles on the floor. Blood-shot eyes and falling over her feet. Jenny was certainly high when they knocked on her door last night. He wishes he can see what liquid she uses to wash all the pills down with.

Michael offers Anthony half a smile, and they shake hands again, "See you for coffee on Monday, and we can talk more about this."

"Sure, first thing."

Michael nods while Anthony greets Vanessa and they part ways.

"I wonder why she went to ER," Vanessa says as they continue to Luc.

"So would I," Michael says when they reach Luc, who is already holding their boat's mooring lines.

"Thanks, Luc," Michael says then gives him a ten-dollar tip.

"My pleasure, Doc."

Michael decides against starting the engine and uses the sails now that a strong wind has picked up. It gives him time to process his thoughts and why Jenny's actions bother him so much.

———

When they arrive at the boathouse, Vanessa gets out first and heads up to their home to make coffee. Michael fastens the boat to the platform and walks up the steps. He looks at their neighbor's house and sees movement. He decides to go over.

He knocks once, no answer. Then knocks a few more times and is about to turn back when the door opens.

"Jenny! Hi."

"Dr. Michael," she croaks, shamefaced when she sees it's him. "What can I do for you today?"

"I just stopped by to see how Gracie is doing? Did you get the medication I prescribed for her?"

"You know what..." Jenny fidgets with her belt buckle, takes a deep breath and continues, "I didn't have anything to give Gracie for her pain, so I decided to go to the hospital pharmacy last night. When we got there, I realized I forgot the script you wrote. So instead of turning all the way back to come get it, I just went to the emergency room. Gracie was so ill and her fever kept spiking. I didn't want to wait." Her smile was quivering.

"Just as long as Gracie is feeling better. Anyway, I won't

keep you. I am at home the rest of the weekend if you need my help?"

Jenny nods. "Thank you for checking up on her. Enjoy your weekend."

"Any time," Michael replies then turns to walk back up to his house.

Jenny closes her front door and locks it.

———

It's Monday morning and Michael arrives early at the hospital. Apart from Jenny and Grace on his mind, he feels relaxed after spending all weekend with Vanessa. He enters the doctor's lounge and finds Anthony with a coffee mug in his hand. They greet and Michael grabs the mug with the name 'Doc M' and fills it with hot coffee. He continues to tell Anthony about the plastic bag full of empty pill bottles at Jenny's house and the reason why she went to the emergency room was because she forgot his prescription at home. He adds his concern that she might be using the medication herself and not treating Grace appropriately. Anthony shares his concerns, and they agree to stay in contact regarding the mother and daughter.

Michael's phone rings, and he fishes it out to answer. It's Olivia Larson's next of kin, requesting permission to have her body removed by the funeral home director.

"As I said, Mr. Larson, you should contact Dr. Orion directly; he is the pathologist for the hospital and will be able to tell you when her body can be released."

Her next of kin mumbles something inaudible and hangs up before Michael can say more. He needs to stop giving out his cell number.

During times of grief, those weeping for a loved one

aren't always thinking properly or comprehend what is said to them. They are busy going through a range of emotions. The stages of grief: the first stage is denial, the person can't believe that someone they love was here one day and gone the next. Anger peeks its nasty head around the corner and those in mourning want to blame someone else for their loss. Then they bargain with the higher power they believe in, beg and plead to bring them back. Then sadness engulfs them and they may experience sleep issues, an increase or decrease in appetite and might need professional treatment. Then, finally, they accept that their loved one isn't coming back, and is in a better place, and try to move on with their life by taking it one day at a time, trying their best to get on without them being around. So much space is left behind; so much time is needed before their loved one is remembered less and less. But, the hurt is still there. The longing is still there. They can never be replaced, no matter how much time passes.

A lump forms in Michael's throat. Not enough time has passed for him to stop thinking about Amelia, their innocent, fragile child. She was so little, relied on them to make her pain go away. To kiss the booboo better. Sometimes, just sometimes, nobody can take any booboo away. Eventually the booboo won and took Amelia away from them, to see her placed inside her tiny coffin and buried. Michael goes to the nearest drinking fountain, where he splashes his face with water, tears a paper towel from the automated machine and dries his face. He needs to get back to work, to his patients' pain.

———

At Penny-Lane, Tanya is going over the weekend report with Michael.

"No casualties, doctor." She smiles at Michael while he reads the report.

He is not overly fond of Tanya; she's rude, has no bedside manner, wears too much make-up and bleaches her hair too often. All the patients complain about her, but, until she does something wrong, he can't get rid of her. Her lips smack while she chews bubble gum.

Michael stops reading and looks up at her. "Do you mind?"

"What?" she asks.

"Bubble gum is not allowed, Tanya." Michael points to the sign hanging on the wall by the nurses' station.

"Oops, I forgot." She laughs and spits the bubble gum into the dustbin next to his foot.

"Please Tanya, I don't want to have to keep reminding you of the rules. These rules are here for a reason, and you should know what they are by now."

"Yes, doctor," she answers, looks down at her hands and smirks.

Michael doesn't want to know what she is thinking about. He continues reading the report.

"Okay, I am going to do my rounds and then I will be going to my consulting rooms." He looks over at Tanya but she is still daydreaming and smiling.

"Okay, Tanya?" Michael says, louder this time.

"Oh yes, Dr. Alastair." She doesn't look him in the eye.

Michael shudders at what her thoughts might be then leaves her at the nurses' station. He starts at room 600, and an hour later he is in the last room, 620, with Edith Cohen – the newest patient to join Penny-Lane. She has been given three months to live due to pancreatic cancer.

"All right, Edith," Michael says to her after reviewing her medical chart, "these changes will help, but let us know."

"Thank you, doctor." She smiles weakly at him.

Michael looks at her food tray. "I will make a deal with you. Eat at least half of your breakfast, and I will smuggle in some chocolate bars for you?"

Edith tries to laugh but it clearly hurts too much. "You remind me of my grandson. He is a doctor too, you know."

"I didn't know that. Does he make deals with you as well?"

She smiles slyly. "Yes." She leans over to her side table and pulls open the drawer. Michael leans over and sees three chocolate bars.

"You should eat one of them." He looks at her with concern.

"I know." She places her hands on her chest, tucks her left hand into her right. "I do like the porridge here." She smiles.

"Here, let me help you." He pushes the button on the hand-held device to move her mattress into an upright position that's comfortable for her. He leans her forward, fluffs her pillows then pulls the food tray closer.

"Some butter?" Michael asks.

She nods and he spoons a small block into the porridge.

"Do you prefer sugar or honey?"

"Honey, please."

Michael takes the honey jar and pours in two full teaspoons which he stirs in.

"You are something different, Dr. Alastair." Edith blurts.

"How so?"

"Well. First of all, when has a doctor performed the job of a nurse? I have been in and out of hospital so many times, and you are the first doctor to show such compassion."

"I will take that as a compliment, Edith." He smiles at her. "If I can help relieve some of your pain, I will do my best." He pushes the food tray right in front of her, making it easier for her to reach the bowl so she can eat.

"Thank you." She wipes tears from her eyes.

He gives her a comforting smile then goes toward the door.

"Edith, let me know if you need anything. I am heading to my consulting rooms in a few minutes. Call Nurse Tanya to get hold of me if you need to."

"Will do, thanks doctor."

———

Michael is halfway through his consulting day when his receptionist buzzes him. He apologizes to the beefy man sitting on the treating bed and goes to answer the phone.

"Yes, I have a patient with me."

"Dr. Alastair, sorry to disturb you, but it's Penny-Lane," Mrs. Jones says into the receiver, sounding heavyhearted.

"What's wrong?"

"I am putting you through to Tanya."

Michael hears a beep then Tanya speaks, "Dr. Alastair?"

"Yes, Tanya, what is it?"

"It's Doc Walsh. He is gone."

Michael can hear Tanya crying on the other end. If he remembers correctly, this is Tanya's first death while alone on duty.

"Okay, Tanya, give me five minutes with my patient, and I will see you upstairs."

"Thank you, doctor." She hangs up.

Michael turns to his patient in order to conclude the consultation.

Ten minutes later, Michael arrives at Penny-Lane with Tommy waiting for him in room 618, the white card in the see-through holder on the door frame.

"Tommy, where is Tanya?" Michael asks when he reaches Tommy at the doorway.

"I d-don't know. She called me after she spoke to you and told me to get up here pronto and to wait here until you came. When I got up here, she was nowhere to be found."

They enter Herbert's room together and find his lifeless body on his bed. His head is turned toward the window, the sunlight shining on his face. Out of habit, Michael checks for a pulse, but he knows the answer.

Three hours earlier Michael emptied the vial for Herbert into a drinking glass and sat it down next to him on the bedside table. Then he politely requested that he only drink the contents in two hours' time – to ensure Michael was not around. Michael then took the empty vial with him and disposed of it in one of the waste dustbins.

Now, standing at the foot of Herbert's bed, Michael reaches for his medical folder and starts writing the standard notes for Dr. Orion. When done, Michael turns to Tommy, who has been waiting patiently beside him. "Tommy, you can take him down to Dr. Orion now. I will wait on the floor until Nurse Tanya gets back."

Michael lifts the sheet and covers Herbert's face.

Tommy does as asked, unlocks the wheels of the bed, places the medical folder on the deceased's body, and begins wheeling him to the elevator. Michael goes to the nurses' station to call Tanya's cell phone from the hospital landline. Her phone goes straight to voice mail. He leaves her a message to come back to the floor as soon as possible. As he puts down the receiver, his cell phone rings.

"Hello?"

"Dr. Alastair, it's Simon. I just received a distraught call from Tanya. Who died at Penny-Lane?"

"Hi, Simon, it was Herbert. What else did Tanya say?"

"Just that she couldn't handle all the death, and through tears said she can't come back and then she hung up."

"Okay. Can either Harriet or yourself come in until I find out whether she will ever come back, and then I will let Dianne know?"

"Can you ask Dianne whether we can hire two new nurses, even if they are junior? The more staff available, the easier it will be on us oldies."

"Not sure, but I will find out."

"Great, thanks, doctor. I will come through. Give me fifteen minutes."

"Thanks, Simon." Michael hangs up.

He shakes his head when he can't get through to Tanya. Her phone is off, but he can still leave a message. How can she just leave the patients like this? He picks up the receiver again and dials Dianne's number in personnel.

———

Michael arrives home before 8pm.

Just in time, thinks Vanessa as she retrieves the pot roast from the oven and begins carving slices.

"Hmmm that smells heavenly." Michael enters the kitchen and greets Vanessa with a tender hug that lasts longer than usual.

"Honey, what's wrong?"

"The doctor passed away this morning. Tanya found him and freaked out. She won't be coming back."

"Good riddance. To Tanya; not your patient." She gives him a smile then leans in for a kiss. "How are you holding up?"

"As good as can be, I suppose. I was expecting it, but it was rougher than usual." He goes to the dining room table, where he sits down at the head.

"It was just one of those days." She raises a plate in his direction, he nods, and she adds a generous amount of meat, as well as four small roast potatoes, a large spoon of corn and another of beans. She sets his plate in front of him, leans down, and kisses him on his head.

"Thanks, Essa. This is just what I need."

Vanessa dishes up her food then sits on his right.

"Finn fetched the artwork today," she pipes up.

"And, what did The Finn say?" Michael teases.

"He loves it, of course." She smiles.

"Of course." He smirks.

She smiles lovingly, takes another bite then adds, "I saw the neighbor."

Michael looks up mid-chew. "Oh. Did she speak to you?"

"No. She was outside with her daughter. They were just walking around in the sun. The little girl is very cute. She was laughing and throwing grass in her hair. It was lovely to watch."

Michael places his knife on his plate and takes Vanessa's hand in his, lifts it and kisses it.

"Anything else happen?" Michael asks.

"No, they were just waiting for the delivery guy. When he arrived, he gave Jenny a huge package and left. Then Jenny and Grace went back inside. Oh, then I heard Gracie cry once they were inside, but she stopped after a few minutes."

———

Jenny sits Grace on the floor beside her and uses the kitchen scissors to open the large package. One of her regular donors messaged her through Facebook Messenger that he would like to send her something for Grace. Jenny refuses to give out her cell phone number or her address, and therefore insists on the number for the courier company and she will contact them herself with the delivery arrangements.

"Gracie, look here, someone bought us something big."

Grace claps her hands and laughs at her mother, who is sitting on the floor with her. Jenny takes a sip of her wine and sets her glass to one side, pulls open the side of the box to reveal a large doll house with all the little accessories.

"Wow! Look, Gracie, it's our very first doll house."

Jenny removes the box from the courier's packaging and opens it. Grace wobbles toward her mother, leans on her shoulder to keep steady.

"Mine?" Grace says as she plonks down next to her mother, almost sitting on Jenny's lap.

"Yes, yours, Gracie."

Jenny opens the box and pulls the doll house out and starts unboxing the accessories. The miniature beds, couches, tables, chairs, television, cupboards. Grace wants to help and tries to take the boxes from her mother's hand.

Frustrated by the tugging, Jenny smacks Grace's little hand and yells, "No, Grace, no snatching! Mommy will give you one. Here, open this box." Jenny gives her the box containing the little fruit bowl that goes on the miniature dining room table.

Grace, a little stunned by the smack, begins to cry.

"You asked for it, Grace. Mommy told you no but you still tried to take it out of my hand. Stop crying."

The louder Jenny speaks, the louder Grace cries. Irritated with Grace's crying, Jenny gets up and throws the box with the little bedroom cupboards on the floor. It bounces up and hits Grace in the face, leaving a tiny paper cut on her cheek. Grace starts shrieking while she holds her cheek, tears streaming down her face.

Jenny gets back down on her knees and starts yelling, "Stop crying, Grace. Stop it! Stop it! Stop it now!"

Jenny starts shaking Grace, but the backward and forward motion causes Grace to sob uncontrollably, and she starts choking on her tears and spit.

Jenny continues, "Why did you do that Grace? What is wrong with you?" Jenny stops shaking Grace, then as calmly as she can, she says, "One, two, three, four..."

It is not working.

Holding her ears closed with her index fingers, Jenny yells, "Shush, Grace. My head!"

Jenny goes into the bathroom and closes the door. She opens the medicine cabinet, selects two pill bottles, and takes one pill out each which she then swallows. She sits on the edge of the bath and starts counting, "One, two, three, four, five, six, seven, eight, nine, ten." She unlocks the bathroom door and goes back into the lounge. Grace is still crying, coughing up saliva. Jenny picks up her wine glass and downs what is left. The she lifts Grace and holds her head against her chest, her own tears mixing with the child's.

"I'm sorry, it's okay, Gracie. I didn't mean to. Shhh..."

Jenny rubs her back softly, kisses her forehead and chants, "It's okay." Jenny kisses her little cheeks. "It's okay," Jenny says, calming Grace and herself in the process.

Jenny sits on the couch with Grace still in her arms. She starts rocking until Grace falls asleep.

During the commotion she didn't notice an envelope fall out the box. Seeing it now, lying on the carpet next to the unopened accessory boxes, Jenny puts Grace on the couch next to her and leans over to pick up the card.

For you Gracie, all my Love. Daddy.

"Ugh!" Jenny says through gritted teeth as she tears up the card and throws it in the courier packaging for discarding. She turns to face Grace, rubs her little back and whispers softly, "Your so-called daddy didn't want you in the beginning, and when you were born, he left you. Now he is trying to make up for it by sending me money and giving you gifts. Now what am I supposed to do with it? It's too beautiful to throw out. I can't throw it out." Jenny sits on the floor and starts putting the doll house together with all the accessories while muttering under her breath, "He probably wants to know where we are and come see you, and then he will want to see you more often. I will not let that happen. You are mine and I will not let that happen." She picks up the larger pieces of the torn card and tears it into smaller pieces.

———

Grace is fast asleep on Jenny's shoulder.

Jenny keeps rubbing her nose but the strong smell of the hospital cleaning fluid still burns her nostrils.

An older nurse walks up to where they are sitting and informs her, "Dr. Jeffreys will see you now, Mrs. Mason. Please follow me."

Jenny stands up with Grace still clinging to her. They follow the nurse into a consulting room marked with a number six.

"Mrs. Mason," Dr. Anthony Jeffreys says to her when she enters. "What's the matter with Grace today?"

"Dr. Jeffreys, I don't know. One moment she was fine, the next she is turning blue and purple. But she is asleep now. I brought her in to the ER as quickly as I could."

"Place her on the bed for me here." Dr. Jeffreys pats the bed beside him and picks up his stethoscope.

While Grace sleeps, Dr. Jeffreys does the necessary checks. He sees a red mark on the left side of her neck, cheek and shoulder.

"Did she have something around her neck or did she fall on her left-hand side?"

"No, not that I know of? She was out of my sight for a moment when I went to the bathroom."

"She has a slight temperature, but other than the red marks, she seems fine. Did she complete the course of antibiotics I prescribed the last time I saw her?"

"Yes, doctor."

"If you want, we can keep her overnight?"

"Yes, please, doctor. I think let's do that, just to make sure she's okay."

"How are you holding up with the unpacking and settling in?" the doctor asks while he writes Grace's script for the pediatric ward.

"Everything is fine, thank you, doctor." She bites on her lower lip and tucks loose strands of soft hair behind her ear. "I see you are on Facebook. Would you mind if I added you to my daughter's page?"

"Your daughter has her own page?"

"Of course. I use it to keep in contact with her sponsors." Jenny takes a step back.

"Thanks for the offer, but I don't think that would be appropriate, Mrs. Mason," he says.

"Oh, none of her other doctors had an issue with it," she replies. "I didn't mean anything by it. Don't worry, I won't bother you with it again." Jenny picks up her daughter. "Are you done? Can we go to the ward now?"

"Sure. I will ask one of the nurses to take you through." Dr. Jeffreys opens the curtain and calls out to a nurse.

———

Vanessa can hear Michael snore all the way from her studio. She shuts the door, hoping it might help. It doesn't. She returns to her workstation, where she mixes a variety of herbs, stems, leaves and flowers she picked early this morning. She thought she would make more than one batch, just in case Michael needs more.

The vials consist of a number of carefully selected ingredients which she mixes together to create the perfect blend. The main ingredient is Atropa belladonna, commonly known as deadly nightshade. The main effects of this plant include hallucinations, dilated pupils and blurred vision, and it has a bitter berry aftertaste. She then adds a pinch of Narcissus, otherwise known as daffodils, for a numbing effect. Some Datura, angel's trumpets, which provide a sense of euphoria. And, lastly, some honey, to give it that natural sweet taste.

Vanessa mixes the ingredients together, pressing them with her marble mortar and pestle until only the oils are left. She has mastered the art of using the exact amount of each ingredient to ensure the patients don't feel any pain during their final moments, the hallucinations to comfort them, and then when they are ready, it is quick.

She stops what she is doing when she hears the floorboards creak. Michael opens the door slowly, peeks through the tiny opening, and stops when he sees she is looking at him.

"I can't sneak up on you anymore. These floorboards give me away." He chuckles.

"You know I hate frights." She lifts an eyebrow. "What if I had a knife in my hand and swipe it at you, slice your delicate soft hands?"

"Well, it's a good thing you heard me coming then." He comes to her, wraps his arms around her shoulders. "What are you busy with so late at night?"

"Tweaking the batch a little, improving it, so to speak." She pats his arms.

"Just like Nana used to. Remember the day I met her, she made me some of that horrible truth-serum tea?" Michael unhooks his arms and sits on the chair beside her.

"I remember. She heard stories about you and wanted to know more."

Michael says, "Yeah, like I was some kind of criminal."

"She wanted to know the truth. You know how kids can be, bending the truth to suit their lies." Her lips curl upward.

"I always tell the truth, you know that."

"I know that," she interjects. "Besides, it didn't hurt, and it worked, didn't it? She knew it wasn't you who destroyed her garden, and she liked you after that day."

"It was embarrassing, borderline emasculating." He chuckles.

"Why are you up so late?" She asks with concern.

"Couldn't sleep, and there was an empty space next to me."

"I'm finished." Vanessa dusts the bits of leaves and stems from her gloves, empties the marble bowl into a bottle, and closes it tightly. She removes her gloves, sets them neatly beside the bottle on the workstation, and washes her hands.

"All done." She stands up, takes his hand. "Come, doctor, let's go sleep."

———

Harriet is flapping her mouth so much Michael wants to block his ears. She is complaining about Simon's tardiness again.

"The replacement nurses can only start tomorrow. You two need to get along." Michael grunts. Not only is he their superior, but their referee as well. "When Simon comes in this afternoon, I will have a word with him, okay?"

"Thank you. That's all I wanted. He needs to grow up." Harriet dusts imaginary sand off her hands.

"Okay, Harriet, it goes for you as well." Michael raises his eyebrows. "I have a full day today and need to get going." He signs the last report then heads to the elevator, where he pushes the button then turns to face her. "Have a good day."

"You too, Doc." She smiles, flashing her yellow teeth.

He notices she is missing her top right premolar and wonders if that happened recently.

———

Harriet finishes her rounds on Penny-Lane then sits at the nurses' station to enjoy her midmorning tea. She slides her tongue over her teeth and to the recent gap. She knows better than to start a fight. It's safer to leave the bastard alone to watch his sports than provoke him. She snaps out of her thoughts then starts reading one of those celebrity gossip magazines. Out the corner of her eye, four patients cross the corridor and go into one room so she glances up.

———

Molly Sims, Mike Fields and Moira Myers tip toe to Edith Cohen's room. The three patients just sit down when Oliver Martinez enters; they all swing their heads in the direction of the door. Mike rubs his neck from the sudden movement.

"Oliver, you almost gave me a heart attack," whispers 86-year-old Edith, clutching her chest with both hands. "We are fragile. Don't sneak up on us like that."

"I wasn't sneaking up on you. I am closer to a hundred than you are, and my left leg drags." He grunts.

Molly, Mike and Moira giggle; they haven't had so much fun in weeks.

"So? What are the four of you whispering about before I interrupted you?" Oliver inches in closer to the group, leaning with his left hand on his walking stick while he holds onto the table with his right to keep his balance.

"We can't tell you," remarks Molly. "How do we know you aren't going to go tell?"

"What? Are we in grade school? I am not a snitch." Oliver lifts his right hand with only his index and middle fingers standing at attention. The others are curled into his hand. "I swear." He moves closer to the others. "Now tell me, what's going on?"

"All right, you can hear," Edith continues in a whisper. "Before Doc Walsh passed away, I heard him call Dr. Alastair to his bedside and say the same words Olivia said. They said. 'I want to dance in the shade of the night' and then a couple of days later they were dead. Do you think it means, what I think it means, that he assists somehow? You know, when you are ready to go to the Big Man in the sky?"

"These walls are so thin. I heard that too," replies Moira. "Before Mr. Jensen moved into room 612, the old lady who was there said the same thing to Dr. Alastair the one day, and the next day she was dead. So yeah, I think when you are ready, you say that sentence to him, and he helps you somehow." She waves her hands up at the ceiling.

"That's illegal," Mike pipes up with a shocked expression.

"Of course it's illegal," Moira confirms.

"I thought everyone dies here naturally..." Mike adds, his last word trailing off as he stares out the window.

"Some do, Mike, but I think some get to a point where their bodies are done but their minds are still awake, and then they are stuck with one foot in the grave.," Edith says, more to herself than to the group in her room.

Now, focusing on each of their faces, Edith continues, "Wouldn't you want some help? If it was offered to you, would you?" She gazes into their eyes. When no one answers her, she continues, "I am eighty-six. My husband died fifteen years ago. I had one child who was killed in a car accident and her useless son doesn't bother to see me. So, if I get to that point, I will call in that cute doctor and whisper that line in his ear. Then, when he leaves, I will smack his bottom for old time's sake." She giggles.

"Edith, contain yourself!" Moira says to her friend and gives her a light smack on her hand. Serious now, she adds,

"Would you? Ask for assistance? Really?" Moira scrunches up her face to reveal her life's worth of wrinkles.

"Of course I would." Edith nods. "If I start shitting and pissing in my bed, I would. If I can't keep food down, if the painkillers don't work anymore and neither does my body. Yeah. Sure. I will be the next one in line. Wouldn't you?" Edith responds a little more aggressively than she wants to but she has to put her point across. Then she adds, a little more gently, "Nobody likes suffering, Moira. You of all people should know this."

Moira looks down when the tears flow down her cheeks, and she doesn't wipe them away. Edith knows how Moira's husband was involved in a serious car accident, suffered a spinal cord injury and lost his right foot. After that, he endured so much pain that he took his own life while Moira was out shopping with their young son. She understands her friend's pain and knows her concerns come from a good place.

Moira nods and takes the tissues Edith offers. "I see where you are going with this. It is still wrong, Edith."

"Well," says Molly, "this is bloody depressing!" She too wipes a tear from her eye.

Edith smiles and gives her a tissue as well.

Molly continues, "Okay. At least we know now. Do it! Don't do it! It's up to personal choice, I say. Each to his own, all right." She nods as she says this. "Just promise me this, if you do decide – do not tell me. Just say goodnight like we always do. If I know it's your last night, I will over-think it and try talk you out of it, 'cause that's how selfish I am." She says the last with a grin.

The ladies nod in unison, move in closer to each other and share hugs. The two men watch them.

Mike pipes up, "Well, I think it's noble of Dr. Alastair.

He knows it's illegal, yet he is compassionate about the whole process. He is a good doctor and doesn't want anyone to suffer. I like him more now."

"Excuse me!" Oliver says. "He is a doctor. He said the Hippocratic Oath which is 'First, do no harm'. So if he is hurting his patients, he needs to be stopped." He folds his arms, squeezing them close to his chest as his frown deepens.

"Oliver, shut up. You don't know what you are talking about," Edith interjects. "Have you ever heard anyone complain? Dr. Alastair helps people die on their own terms and with dignity. And, besides, have you ever heard any of those who have passed scream in pain while they die?"

Oliver shakes his head and looks at his slippers. "No."

Edith sits up in bed. "Well, all I am going to say is we don't know what really happens, and we will not say a word about this again. What if we are wrong and we end up destroying a doctor's life?" She eyeballs everyone in her room. "Does everyone understand me?"

They all nod, with a few yeses going around the room.

"Now get to your own rooms. I need to rest." She waves them away.

———

Michael and Mrs. Jones are reviewing his diary for the following day when Anthony enters the room.

"Michael," he announces.

"Anthony, what can I do you for?" Michael looks up at him.

"Can I see you in your room quickly?" Anthony tilts his head toward Michael's office and goes there.

Michael nods. "I will be right there." He turns back and

says to his assistant, "Thanks, Mrs. Jones. Tomorrow seems fine. Just swop those two around, and then I will see you in the morning." He smiles at her then heads for his office, where he shuts the door.

Anthony starts, "Mrs. Mason came in again last night with Grace."

"What was wrong?"

"Grace presented with a temperature, and she had red marks on the left side of her neck, cheek and shoulder. I admitted her for observation and sent her for X-rays, a scan and a full blood work-up. And guess what?" Anthony pauses for effect, and Michael shakes his head. "They all came back normal. I couldn't find anything wrong with Grace."

"And then?"

"I discharged her this morning. There was no reason to keep her in the ward. I told Mrs. Mason to come by, should she get worse again."

"Jenny did mention seizures and ear infections?" Michael says, more as a statement than a question.

Anthony shakes his head. "I couldn't find anything wrong with Grace."

"Did you prescribe any take-home medication?"

"The usual for pain," Anthony says. "Do you think Jenny is doing this to get Grace's medicine?"

Michael nods.

———

Michael arrives at the nurses' station the next morning only to find it deserted. Not again.

He calls for Harriet and Simon; nobody answers.

He calls again, then Simon sticks his head out of room 602, calls Michael over.

"It's Oliver Martinez, Dr. Alastair," whispers Simon.

"What's wrong?"

"Don't think he is going to make it."

"Let me see him."

Michael enters Oliver's room where Harriet is busy with his vitals, and the two new nurses watch intently.

How quickly everything can change. The day before Oliver was walking around and cracking jokes, today he is a frail old man with a gaunt face. He watches him struggle to drink water through a straw. He sees Michael, lifts his hand, and with his index finger calls Michael over.

Michael goes to his bedside and leans in with his ear to Oliver's mouth.

"I am ready to go, doctor. Please help me. Please make it painless." Tears gather in Oliver's eyes, reflecting his pain.

Michael knows what Oliver is asking, but he needs to hear the words, the sentence. The sentence that started everything. The sentence his daughter said when she was so ill, when she was too tired to eat or drink or walk. She asked him, her own father to help take the booboo away, to help her sleep forever. She was still so young. How could he do such a thing? How could he help her? He wanted her to live; he wanted her to stay with them for as long as possible. He couldn't help her. He hadn't. When the time eventually came, she was barely there. Thinking back, he should have helped her when she needed him, when she asked, when she said the sentence. The words from her favorite book, about a young patient who, to alleviate the pain, leaves the hospital at night and is magically transported to another place where she is able to dance under the stars, in the shade of the night, pain free.

He whispers something into Oliver's ear then sits back

up to look him in the eyes. Oliver mumbles and Michael leans in again with his ear to his mouth.

In a whisper he confirms, "Yes doctor, I want to dance in the shade of the night."

Michael sits back up, pats Oliver's hands that lie still on his chest, and nods.

"Everybody, please get out," Michael says sternly.

Harriet stays put.

"You too, Harriet," Michael adds, walks to the door and holds it open for them as they leave.

"What are you going to do, doctor?" Harriet asks as she exits.

"His dying wish is for peace. I am honoring that wish." Michael shuts the door and locks it.

Ten minutes later, Michael opens the door, as white as a sheet.

"Someone call Tommy, please."

"Are you all right?" Harriet asks as he approaches them.

"Yes, I will be fine. Please call Tommy. He needs to take Oliver's body down to Dr. Orion."

"What happened?" Harriet asks.

"Oliver wanted to die without so many people gawking at him."

Harriet looks down and blushes.

Michael is still gazing at her when she looks up again. Their eyes meet and she turns her head away from him.

"A moment please, Harriet." Michael goes to the far end of the corridor. Harriet follows him.

"I didn't want to ask this in front of everyone else, but are you all right?" Michael lifts his finger and points to her left cheek. "You never wear makeup, but you are today and it has smudged a little."

"Oh dear." She frets, covers her cheek with her hands. Tears gather in her eyes.

"Your husband?" he asks.

The bruises on her cheek were caused by a hard punch to the bone, just missing her eye.

Harriet nods. "He has been good at not hitting my face, except this last time." She pulls out a tissue and dries her eyes, careful not to smudge the rest of the foundation.

"How long has this been going on?"

"Since he lost his job."

"Two years?"

She nods, looks at her feet again.

He never realized what she was going through and never stopped to ask. She had hid her troubles well until he hit her in the face. He tries to make light of the situation and offers a gentle diagnosis, "It looks like it's only a bruise, nothing serious and should clear in a couple of weeks."

"Yes, doctor." Her smile is weak.

"Can you leave him?" He asks.

She shakes her head. "No, the mean ass says he will kill me and the girls."

She looks him in the eye. "I wish there was another way to get rid of him." She blows her nose.

Michael doesn't answer. He thinks of ways in which she can get away from someone as possessive and dangerous as her husband. Divorce, restraining order, arrest. All legal possibilities.

"I know what you do for them, here at Penny-Lane." Harriet keeps her eyes focused on his, doesn't blink.

She whispers, "I know, doctor. I know how you help these patients. I saw you with Allan, Fran and more recently with Moira. I heard what they said to you, to let you know what they want. I won't say anything to anyone about it, but you must help me, please." She leans in closer. "I have to get rid of that monster soon before he kills me." More tears stream down her face.

"If you know, then you must understand why I can't help you with your husband. Not in that way. We can find a way legally, but I can't help you the way you want."

"Please, just one vial?"

———

Michael asks Mrs. Jones to cancel the rest of his afternoon appointments. The entire morning while he tends to his patients, he keeps thinking of Harriet and her problem, what she is asking of him. He feels sorry for her, what she is going through, what her daughters are going through. He sees himself as an angel of mercy, not as a killer by proxy.

When he writes a prescription for a patient, he sees her tears.

When he listens to a heart murmur, her words beat on.

Over and over again, all morning long.

The only thing he could say to Harriet is that he will think about it and then he left her standing there. She is desperate, and he, of all people, understands that when one is backed into a corner like he is, like she is – desperate measures call for desperate actions. He has been so careful, but it doesn't matter now; she knows and she wants a vial. What does he say to Vanessa? She warned him. After the first few – she warned him, and warned him again a week ago. She told him so. He sits in his chair with his head in his hands. For the first time in a long while he doesn't know what to do.

At two o'clock he orders Mrs. Jones to go home, and at

three he leaves. He wants to go straight home. He can't face Harriet now, not so soon anyway. He decides to send Simon a text message, even though he isn't the one on duty at the moment. He explains that he is unable to attend the afternoon rounds and will be in tomorrow morning. They can call him on his cell if they need him.

The drive home goes too quickly, barely enough time for him to think. It takes him less than twenty-five minutes driving on autopilot until he parks outside his garage door. He sits in his car with it still idling for what feels like an eternity. That is, until Vanessa knocks on his window.

"Are you okay? You know if you are trying to kill yourself, you aren't doing a very good job?" She chuckles at her joke, her curly brown hair neatly tied back with a few loose strands.

Michael doesn't respond.

"What's wrong?" she asks, tries to open his car door but it's locked. "Michael, open the door." She starts banging on his window.

Michael turns off the engine and unlocks the car. Vanessa opens his door and steps out of his way when he climbs out.

"What is it? You are frightening me."

"Harriet knows!"

"She knows? Are you sure? How do you know?"

"She asked for a vial."

"What?"

"Her husband is abusive and threatening her, and she wants to get rid of him." He gives her the look.

"Oh no, poor dear. Her poor children."

"Exactly."

"How long?"

"About two years."

"You never suspected?"

"No," he says, shrugging. "I already feel guilty for not noticing what she was going through."

"Give her one. If she wants it, give her one."

Shocked by his wife's response, he retorts, "What? We are killing a man, her husband – an evil one, but still. We are supplying her with the murder weapon, and we are accessories to his murder."

Vanessa lowers her voice. "Hun, Harriet has been working with you for so many years, and only raising it now out of sheer desperation, it tells me she will continue to keep your secret. 'Cause, guess what, you will be keeping one of her secrets too. She wants to get rid of her horrible husband, so let her. She can't tell on you without spilling the beans on herself."

"I thought you would be angry at me?" he confesses.

"Angry at you? What on earth for?"

"You warned me. You said to be careful, that someone might see me."

"No, I am not angry. It's Harriet." She leans in to hug him.

"And –"

"And... What do you mean by...and?" Vanessa says.

"And one of my patients died."

"Us?"

"No, he did ask – he said the sentence. He was so close to dying, and I knew it wouldn't be long. Instead I chased everyone out of his room while I stayed with him and gave him some morphine for the pain and held his hand until he passed away. It took about ten minutes."

It reminds Michael of that dark time, sitting around their daughter's bed, each holding one of her hands, her fragile little body struggling to hold on. How she opened her eyes and looked at them, whispered that she was dancing in the shade of the night, then closed her eyes for the last time, her little hands going limp in theirs.

Vanessa touches Michael's face tenderly and says, "Give her one of the vials. What will be, will be, my love." She reaches up and kisses him.

———

A sense of serenity washes over Michael the following morning. He stares at the man in the mirror with satisfaction; that yesterday one of his patients didn't need his help, only a comforting hand. Not forgetting that it is possible he might lose his medical license and go to prison. But, he won't think about that now. Today he will give Harriet a vial and she can do with it as she pleases.

He sees her at the nurses' station playing sudoku on her phone, her foundation still layered on her face. He props the vial in front of her and tells her to discard of the bottle when she's done. She takes the vial, nods, and hides it in her handbag then continues playing her game. That is it. Feeling strangely calmer than before, Michael continues on his rounds. He sees the three recently vacated beds available for new occupants, and makes a mental note to contact Dr. Samuels. As Michael is about leave, Simon arrives, ready to take over from Harriet. He watches her as she jumps up from her chair, and with a spring in her step, she leaves. Michael has never seen her so happy in all the years they have worked together, and he smiles.

———

The weekend passes without any incident at Penny-Lane. On Monday morning, Michael and Anthony meet up again for coffee to discuss the various cases each is working on. Dr. Samuels greets the two men in the lounge and informs Michael that he has two patients who will be transferring to Penny-Lane for continued compassionate care. Michael can feel today is going to be good.

———

"I don't know what happened; she just started vomiting and convulsing. Is she okay? Is my baby going to be okay?" Jenny cries as one of the emergency nurses tries to push her out of the way.

"Ma'am, Dr. Jeffreys is with her to insert a drip."

"A drip, why?"

"She is dehydrated, ma'am. Now, please sit over here," the nurse in charge says to her and points to the row of chairs in the waiting area. "I will fetch you when he is done and she is ready to be moved into the pediatric ward."

"Okay." Jenny does as she is told, and goes to one of four chairs in the waiting area, where she sits down. She opens her bag, feels around for a bottle and removes four tablets that she swallows without any water. She takes out her phone and taps on the Facebook application, scrolls to the Save Gracie Page.

My Gracie is in hospital again. She started vomiting this morning and has a terrible fever :-(It's not looking good. Please keep her in your prayers.

She presses the Post button.

After a few seconds, the first few likes highlight her screen and she smiles. She looks up when she hears the door open, and Dr. Jeffreys exits her daughter's room. He walks directly toward her, and she rises when he reaches her.

"Mrs. Mason." He holds out his hand, and she shakes it firmly. "I inserted a drip because she is severely dehydrated. Has she been able to hold any liquids down?"

"No. When I changed her diaper this morning, it was a runny mess. I know, she needs to come off diapers, but she still needs to wear them during the night," Jenny replies, knotting her fingers together as she speaks. "She asked for her bottle which I gave her, then the rest of the day she refused to drink anything else, and then she started vomiting, shaking and when she went purple, I knew I had to bring her in. Can I see her now?"

"She is sleeping at the moment, but you can go to her. We are going to move her to the pediatric ward in a few minutes. You can walk with when we do."

"Great." Jenny wants to run, but thinks better of it and walks quickly. She opens the door and finds her daughter in a fetal position, asleep on the bed. Her soft, innocent features remind her of herself at that age. She smiles to herself then goes to Grace, kisses her delicate cheek and runs her fingers through her soft hair. Grace opens her eyes and lifts her sore hand, revealing a one-size-fits-all drip with a plaster to keep it in place. Jenny takes her little hand in hers and kisses the booboo.

"The doctors will help you. They will make you feel better." Jenny kisses her cheek again and pulls the covers over her tiny body.

Grace closes her eyes as she snuggles with the little brown teddy bear. Jenny brings out her phone and takes a picture of Grace, and posts it on Facebook.

My poor Gracie, she isn't doing well!

The Save Gracie page with the new picture of Grace

and the teddy is shared by twenty people and there are thirty-seven likes already. Jenny gets that warm feeling knowing that people out there care so much about her...and about her Gracie. A personal message pops up and it's him, asking what is wrong with her, and can he see her. She deletes the message.

A tune chimes, a new text message has come through; it's the third time she is receiving such a message and she rolls her eyes. She replies, 'When I get paid'.

Everybody needs to just back off. Everybody wants a piece of her all the time. If it's not Gracie who craves her attention constantly it's those guys who keep sending her text messages; she will pay them when she can. Or it's her baby daddy with his constant irritating questions. She wishes everybody could just leave her alone. In peace. Jenny digs in her bag for her bottles and takes out two tablets.

Dr. Jeffreys comes in as Jenny returns her phone to her back pocket. "The nurses are going to move Grace now."

"Thank you, Dr. Jeffreys."

———

Jenny is sitting in the visitors' chair beside Grace's bed. It's around 7am and all the machines connected to Grace start sounding. Jenny sits up to watch all the machines go off like Christmas lights. A robust nurse with large hands enters the room and shoos Jenny out. She can hear them yelling, but she doesn't care what they say. Dr. Jeffreys runs down the corridor toward her, but he doesn't greet her as he enters Grace's room, he brushes past her as if she is nothing and closes the door behind him. Jenny takes out her phone and opens Facebook. She types a post about what just happened, asking everyone to pray for her...to pray for

Gracie. Jenny decides to get some coffee and sees the machine near the waiting area. She presses the espresso button twice then hot gooey liquid drips out. When it finishes, she picks it up and tastes it. Not too bad, considering how awful it looks. She takes another sip.

Jenny waits at least forty minutes before Grace's door finally opens and Dr. Jeffreys comes out; she can see he is looking for her – she gets up and goes to him.

"Dr. Jeffreys, how is Gracie?"

"Mrs. Mason, do you know what happened in there?"

"No? Why?" She shakes her head, shrugs. "Is she okay?"

"She went into cardiac arrest. When I checked up on her about two hours ago, she was fine, then an hour later she almost dies." The man pales.

"Is she going to be okay, doctor?" Jenny asks.

"She is stabilized. You can't go in there just yet. The nurses are busy cleaning the room. When they are done, you can see her."

"Okay."

"The nurse will call you when they are ready." He wipes sweat off his forehead with his handkerchief.

Jenny notices the quality of it, something only rich people have, and sees his initials are sewn into it as well. She rolls her eyes as she turns toward the nurses' station to wait.

Before the doctor leaves, he asks, "I need to file some paperwork and will be down in ten minutes. Will you wait for me?"

"Yes, of course."

———

Anthony sits at his desk, and Michael is standing next to it. Both are watching the screen.

"I can't believe this, Anthony," Michael says, crossing his arms. His jaw clenches tighter while he watches the video. "I can't believe it. Where is she now?"

Anthony eventually pries his eyes away from the screen and looks up at Michael. "We should have seen this coming."

"We didn't know, and we have proof," Michael responds, wiping his eyes with his hands. "Call security."

Anthony picks up his phone, dials nine and speaks, but Michael is too stunned to register what is said.

When Anthony hangs up, he says to Michael, "They are on their way. Let's go."

———

Jenny types the following onto the Save Gracie page and hits post.

> Dear Facebook friends, my Gracie couldn't hold on any longer.
> Heavenly Angels have taken her away from me :'-(
> Funeral donations welcome.

She adds a link with her bank details and another personal message pops up. This she deletes without reading. Then she digs in her bag for pill bottles and swallows four more.

———

The elevator takes longer than usual; after waiting two minutes they decide to take the stairs. Anthony enters the pediatric ward first, still out of breath, and he starts searching for Jenny.

There is a nurse in Grace's room and another at the nurses' station; he goes into Grace's room first to see that she is safe and stable.

He turns to speak to the nurse. "Nurse Jenkins, where is Grace's mom?"

"I don't know, doctor. She came in earlier after you left, saw Grace's condition and mumbled something that it was too much for her to handle, and then she left."

"Thanks, stay here and don't leave Grace's side. Please, it's important." He points to Grace's bed. "And keep the door locked, and do not let her mother inside."

Michael searches the ward and stops outside Grace's door when Anthony comes out. "I don't see her," Michael says, catching his breath. Two security guards approach them.

"Dr. Jeffreys," says the first guard sternly, "where is the mother?"

"Not here. Go to the control booth and check the exit and entrance footage now, please. I need to know if she is still here."

"Yes, doctor," says the first guard. He pulls out his two-way radio and begins talking.

Anthony says under his breath, "She's gone, Michael. She does this to her child and then leaves her. She could have gone home?"

Michael looks at him. "I can phone Vanessa. She can go have a look and let us know if she is home."

Anthony nods.

———

After breakfast, Vanessa decides to work in her garden. They had a few sprinkles of rain last night, and this morning the weeds show their heads. She prefers her garden neat and weed-free. Just before lunch, she hears commotion from next door. She walks along the side of her house to her front garden and can hear a woman crying. She goes inside her house and takes off her gardening gloves in the kitchen then washes her hands. The telephone rings. It's Michael.

She picks up the container of scones she baked earlier and goes back outside, walks the path. At Jenny's front door, Vanessa can hear loud sobs and rings the doorbell. The sobs stop. Jenny opens the screen door.

"Are you okay?" Vanessa asks.

Jenny's eyes are bloodshot and puffy. She wipes her nose with a tissue. "No." She sobs again, speaks into her hands.

Vanessa leans forward. "Sorry, did you say something happened to Gracie?"

Jenny nods. "Yes, she passed away."

"Ah, you poor thing." Vanessa goes toward the mourning mother and gives her a hug. "Come. Let me make you some tea, and you tell me all about it. I brought scones." Vanessa lifts the container lid for Jenny to see the scones, she opens the door for Vanessa who then locks the door behind them. She puts her right arm around the young mother, and they both go inside her house.

Vanessa seats Jenny at the kitchen table and places the scones in front of her. "Here, you probably haven't eaten much today, if at all. Try them. They are delicious." Jenny's skin is paler than usual, her cheeks sunken, and her finger-nails are chipped.

Jenny shakes her head. "I haven't eaten in two days, I think. I can't remember. Grace has been in hospital and then a couple of hours ago she passed away. My Gracie is gone."

"I am so sorry, Jenny. Do you want to tell me what happened?" Vanessa knows what happened, but she wants to hear it from Jenny. She navigates her way around Jenny's kitchen for cups and puts on the kettle. There are three glass containers: one for coffee, one for tea, and the last for sugar cubes. She picks up the tea container and places a bag into each mug then goes to the fridge for cream.

Jenny continues, "She was so ill and then she just got worse and worse, and then her little body just gave up." She wipes a tear from her eye then draws a deep breath.

A ping sounds from Jenny's phone and she picks it up. Vanessa looks over her shoulder and sees $100 has been deposited into her account. She is already receiving money. Her child isn't even dead, but she is already playing the grieving parent. The kettle starts to whistle then switches itself off.

Vanessa sets the cream on the counter and asks, "Do you take any sugar or cream?"

"One sugar cube and some cream, thanks," Jenny responds meekly.

Vanessa pours the boiled water three quarters of the way into each of the mugs, empties the contents from one of her vials into Jenny's mug then adds two sugar cubes with cream. She removes the tea bag and hands Jenny the mixture. She prefers her tea strong and keeps the bag inside, picks up her mug and sits down next to Jenny.

"Do you need any help with the funeral arrangements?" Vanessa asks, patting the back of Jenny's hand.

Jenny wipes her face, takes one of the scones and bites

into it. "Hmm, this is good." She gives Vanessa a weak smile then washes down the scone with her tea. Jenny pulls a face at the taste. "Did you add sugar?"

"Yes, here, have another cube if it's not sweet enough." Vanessa gets up, adds another sugar cube and hands Jenny the spoon to stir.

Jenny stirs her tea and takes another sip. "That's better. Thank you, Vanessa. I know we hardly know each other, but thank you for this." Jenny motions toward the scones and tea, and offers a sad smile. "I think I should leave and go back to my hometown."

"When are you thinking of leaving?"

"Now. I have already started packing some of my things. I want to go back today." She drinks more of the tea.

"What about Grace's body?"

"I will make the necessary arrangements to have her body collected." Jenny splutters, clears her throat. "Whoa!"

"What's the matter?" Vanessa stands up next to Jenny and pats her on her back. "Are you okay? You don't look well."

Jenny pushes back her chair and tries to rise but she falls into her chair again. She tries to hold onto something next to her but grabs air and crashes to the ground.

"What did you put in my tea?" Jenny asks, clenching her jaw.

"Something you deserve."

Jenny's eyes widen. "What do you mean?"

"The bond between a mother and her child is sacred. A mother is there to protect her baby, no matter what. You were hurting your child, Jenny. A perfect little being, and you were using her for drugs and slowly killing her. Someone like you should never have been able to have a child, let alone look after one." Vanessa shakes her head; she can feel heat rise within her, and her knuckles go white.

"It was an accident!" Jenny grabs her throat.

"There are no accidents for someone like you. Don't worry, Jenny, it will be over soon enough." Vanessa removes her cell phone from her pocket and dials 911. "There is no compassion for you."

Jenny tries to speak, but only a crackling gargling sound comes out of her mouth. She lifts her arms as if protecting herself from something then pushes herself backward. Her head strikes the cupboard and she groans in pain. Vanessa leans in closer to Jenny to hear her, but there is no sound. Jenny just stares at her. Vanessa keeps an eye on her while holding on for the operator; she can see beads of sweat on Jenny's forehead, her skin glow, and her eyes darken.

Vanessa kneels down beside Jenny. "Now you know what it feels like, Jenny. All those times you poisoned Gracie. All those times you hurt her and made her cry. She is your daughter, and you are supposed to protect her from harm. You are supposed to keep her safe and kiss her booboos away, not cause them."

Jenny's eyes widen for the last time, and then her head falls to the side. Vanessa places her shaking index and middle fingers on her neck for signs of life, but there are none. She goes to the front door to unlock and open it then heads to the bathroom to splash water on her face. The heat raging within her quietens down, and she returns to the kitchen and sits on the floor, takes Jenny's hand in hers. She will wait with the body until the paramedics arrive, or her husband, whoever gets here first.

———

Michael arrives first, enters the kitchen and finds Vanessa sitting next to Jenny, still holding her hand.

"Are you okay?" He bends down and kisses the top of her head, helps her up.

She nods.

"We need to make it look like she killed herself."

Wearing gloves, he goes into Jenny's bathroom and finds three prescription bottles in the cabinet and empties them out into the basin and on the floor.

He takes out his cell phone and calls Dr. Orion and informs him of the details.

"Did you find anything else?" Vanessa asks, sitting at the table with her hands clasped. She hasn't moved since Michael helped her into the chair. She keeps looking at the body, expecting it to move. It doesn't.

"Well, the combination of the three prescriptions I found is definitely a lethal mix. No one will suspect anything else."

"How is Grace?" She takes her eyes off a speck of dust to look at her husband when he enters the kitchen.

"She will recover." He sits across the table from her.

"No matter how many times I try to close her eyes, they keep opening." Vanessa looks at the lifeless woman again.

"Dr. Alastair."

They both turn to find the paramedic standing in the doorway.

"It was wide open, so I let myself in."

"Derrick." Michael rises and walks over to him. They shake hands.

"Doc Michael!" says a man standing behind Derrick, blowing vapor fumes into his red hair. Derrick swats the smell away and stands to the side so the brute behind him can pass.

"Detective Daniel Adams!" Michael calls to him, smiling as he approaches. They bear hug each other. "How are you, champ?"

"Good." The detective pats his chest. "I would have been dead if it wasn't for you, so I am doing great!" He smiles at Michael.

He turns to face Vanessa. "Vanessa, my darling, you look wonderful, all considered."

"Flattery will get you everywhere, Daniel." Vanessa rises for a hug, and he squeezes her a little harder than he should. She pats him on the back as an indication for him to let her go.

"Well, what in God's name happened here?" He looks over at the body lying on the floor. "Whats up with her eyes? Can you close them?"

"We have tried, Daniel, but they keep opening." Michael walks around the kitchen table to Jenny's body and tries to close her eyes. They close for a few seconds but open again.

"Ooh!" Daniel pulls his face in disgust when her eyes pop open. "Dr. Orion is on his way. I am going to check the rest of the house." He leaves the kitchen to continue with his investigation.

Vanessa turns to Michael and whispers, "I am not feeling well. If Daniel wants to speak to me, he knows where he can find me."

"Let me walk you out," he says as he walks behind her with one hand on her shoulder.

Once they reach the front door, he hugs her then kisses her forehead. "I will see you in a little bit."

She nods then turns to walk the path back to their home.

Michael enters the house again, passes the kitchen and

sees the paramedic still standing there. He tells him he can leave, since Dr. Orion is on his way. When he goes to the bathroom, he finds Daniel rummaging through Jenny's medicine cabinet.

"Quite the pill popper here, Doc."

"That's not the worst of it."

"Yeah." Daniel stops to look at Michael. "What else?"

"Jenny and her two-year-old daughter, Grace, moved here a few weeks back. I treated Grace one evening, but Jenny went to the hospital anyway and saw Anthony. Then every now and then she would go to hospital because Grace was ill. Anthony treats her; the little girl gets better, then when she is back in her mother's care she gets sick again. At first, we thought Jenny was using her daughter to get her hands on medication, but as it turns out she was also using her daughter for sympathy and attention. I suspect the medication in the bathroom was crushed and given to Grace in her milk or whatever liquid she offered the child. In small-enough doses, the medication is strong enough to give a child seizures, convulsions even high fevers. Basically, she was slowly killing her own child. To make matters worse, she did it at the hospital as well."

"How do you know?" Daniel continues going through the medicine cabinet, reading each label carefully.

"A couple of months ago, Anthony had the hospital insert cameras in all the rooms for training as well as security purposes. After Grace coded, we watched the footage. We saw Jenny ingest a handful of tablets and give Grace her bottle – which we assume had the medication mixed in already."

Daniel stops his search to look at Michael. "That's terrible. How can a mother do that to her own?"

Michael continues, "By the time we called security, she had already left. Luckily, the child is fine."

"What do you call moms like that, that term again? Munch...what?"

"Munchausen syndrome by proxy."

"Yeah, that's it. Sick man, just sick. Do you know whether she got the attention she craved?"

"Anthony says she may have a Facebook page?"

"I will check it out. What was Vanessa doing here?"

"She heard Jenny crying and came over to see what was wrong. She made Jenny tea, then a couple of minutes later Jenny keels over and dies right in front of her. Vanessa says she was in her house barely ten minutes and then this happened."

"Okay, I am sure Dr. Orion will tell us more when he is done with the autopsy. Let me finish up here and then we can go over the details again."

———

Daniel comes over for tea and scones a few days after Jenny's death. Dr. Orion ruled it a suicide, and the case is closed. As Daniel is about to leave, he mentions Jenny's Facebook page and that there are many comments posted about how sick Grace apparently was. "If you ask me, it was Jenny who was sick. After she posted the comment about Grace being dead, she asked for funeral donations and received about $14,000 into her account before we shut it down. Like you said, she was in it for attention, the drugs, and of course the money. Also on her page was Grace's birth, she was legitimately sick then, and Jenny couldn't pay all the medical bills. That's when she created the Save

Gracie page on Facebook and received over $150,000 back then."

"That's terrible, just awful," Michael says.

Vanessa can only shake her head.

"The good news is, we were able to track down the girl's father and he fetched her yesterday. He says he didn't even know about Grace until a year ago. He lost contact with Jenny round about the time she was pregnant, and she just disappeared. Jenny only told him about Grace when she ran out of money, and he has been trying to get hold of her ever since."

"That is good news. I'm glad to hear you were able to find her father." Vanessa gives Daniel a hug.

"Thanks for the scones, but I need to get back."

"Thanks for the update, Daniel." Michael and Vanessa wave him goodbye.

———

With everything settled, and the events of the past few days over, Vanessa still can't sleep and neither can Michael, thanks to Vanessa's insomnia. He rolls over onto his side to face her and places his arm around her waist.

"Are you okay?" Michael asks Vanessa in the quiet of their bedroom.

"I will be. I just keep seeing her face. How her eyes rolled back and the mumbling when she fell onto the floor."

He squeezes her tighter, pulls her toward him, and wedges his head between her head and her shoulder – a perfect fit.

"The first is always the scariest. Over time you will forget, little by little."

"I want to forget now," she says. "Even though it was me

who did that to her, I am glad she is gone, and she can't hurt that little girl anymore."

"No, she won't be hurting anyone anymore."

"I've been meaning to ask you. What happened with Harriet?"

"Her husband had a real heart attack and died." He chuckles. "What are the chances of that happening? She said she threw the contents down the drain and threw the vial away. Thanked me again."

"That's good. Glad we could help without really helping."

She looks up at him, their eyes lock, and they kiss.

Also by N Gray

vinci-books.com/deadlypatterns

When a standard medical procedure ends with a girl missing and another dead, the case lands on Dana Mulder's desk.

Private investigator Dana Mulder faces a deadly web of medical malpractice when a respected doctor's obsession becomes murder. As threats close in, Dana must fight with all she has to reveal the truth.

Turn the page for a free preview

Deadly Pattern: Chapter One

Bianca stretched her legs. That familiar click in her right knee sent a jolt of pain up her leg; the movement caused her to move her upper body, and pain from her shoulder made her wince. She relaxed one muscle at a time, and, after a few seconds, the pain dissipated. Having another scar once she'd healed wasn't comforting, but it was just another scar to add to the one that went down her right leg.

When Bianca had first arrived at the hospital, she had shared a room with another patient before being wheeled into surgery. Now she had a private room and wondered whether her insurance had approved it in full, because she didn't have money to pay the difference should there be an outstanding balance.

Her room was clean with the standard eggshell-colored walls, starched bedding, and repulsive hospital smell—disinfectant mixed with body odor and the lingering stench of a corpse or two.

Her shoulder throbbed, and the joint felt tight. She tried to move it, but it was strapped tightly in a sling against her body. It was an old sports injury that had worsened when she had fallen. She couldn't remember how she had fallen on the sidewalk; she was walking one second, the next thing she had woken in the back of someone's truck. The kind man had offered to take her to the hospital. The next day, she was scheduled for a rotator cuff repair.

Gently massaging against the bandage on her shoulder, she felt something, and wondered whether the orthopedic surgeon had done an arthroscopy as he had promised or if he had gone full on butcher on her arm. She shuddered at the thought.

Footsteps sounded; a light knock on the door was followed by a nurse beaming at Bianca as she entered. "Morning, my name is Mary, and I'll tend to you today. How ya feeling?" The nurse wore a tight white bun on top of her head, had clear crystal-blue eyes, and a warm smile to match her happy demeanor. She carried a blood pressure monitor and reached for Bianca's arm. Her powdery perfume wafted in behind her, causing Bianca to stifle a sneeze.

"Okay, I guess. When will I see the doctor?" Bianca sat up, using her uninjured arm. Her right arm throbbed in the sling as she moved even though she kept it still. She leaned against the pillow, breathless. She could stay where she was. She didn't have the strength to sit all the way upright; that position was as good as it would get.

"He's busy with other patients, but you'll see him soon," Mary said while leaning Bianca forward, fluffed her pillows then helped her lay back again. "You comfy now?"

Bianca nodded. "And my dad, is he here yet?"

"No, but I'll send him in the moment he gets here." Mary squeezed her knee through the starched bedding.

"Don't fret. I'm sure he'll visit you soon." She cocked her head with a sympathetic smile. "You hungry?"

"Not really. Maybe thirsty." Bianca felt blood drain from her face. The sudden movements didn't agree with her, and bile rose, which she swallowed, tasting the bitter aftereffects of the anesthesia.

Mary smiled knowingly. "It's just the morphine. It makes patients a little nauseated soon after the procedure. Don't panic with what I'm about to do." Mary lifted the bleached covers. "I'm just going to remove the catheter."

Bianca felt a gentle tug on her lower body but didn't notice the little tube leaving her. She did have an overwhelming need to urinate though.

Mary unhooked the bag from the side of her bed and placed it on the trolley that stood against the far wall.

Bianca relaxed, hoping the feeling would disappear, but it didn't, and she needed to go. "Okay, I need the bathroom now." Bianca slowly sat upright.

Mary smiled, pulled the covers all the way back and helped her off the bed.

Bianca wobbled slightly, but Mary steadied and guided her to the small bathroom in the corner.

Once Bianca was done and back in bed, Mary left the room but returned after a few seconds, wheeling a trolley full of food and a glass of juice to Bianca's bedside. She set the plate of food onto the over-bed table with cutlery and a plastic cup with three capsules. "Eat." She sat in the chair beside the bed and watched intently.

"Are you going to watch me eat the whole time?" Bianca lifted the lid to see scrambled eggs and toast.

"They say eggs and dry toast go down easier on the first day. Don't mind me. I'm here to ensure you're okay and can eat something before you take your pain meds." She jerked her chin at the plastic cup holding the capsules.

Bianca ate slowly and sipped even slower on the orange juice then paused until the nausea passed before she continued eating.

Mary watched Bianca the entire time. Frosted-colored eyes gleamed at her once she finished. "Now for your medicine, it'll help with the pain. I promise." Mary pushed the plastic cup closer along with the half-full glass of orange juice.

Bianca swallowed one capsule at a time, finishing the orange juice.

Mary removed the plate and glass and handed her the remote for the television against the wall opposite her bed.

She flicked through the channels—all six of them—eventually stopping on a cartoon about a mouse. Bianca's eyelids felt heavy. Her skin tingled, and her body relaxed one muscle at a time. The medication took its hold on her.

When Mary closed the door behind her, Bianca's eyes fluttered open, alarmed when she heard the door shut with a distinct sound of a lock turning.

Bianca's heart hammered against her chest. Why was she locked in?

vinci-books.com/deadlypatterns

About the Author

N Gray is a USA Today Bestselling Author who lives in Cape Town, South Africa with her daughter. During the day she's an analyst and provider profiler for a medical insurance company. At night, she types on her curved keyboard creating fictional characters some may love, and others you want to kill yourself.

She writes in four genres; urban fantasy, thriller, horror and paranormal romance. She now writes under Natalie Michaels for her new thrillers, and SD Syns for her new horrors.

Acknowledgments

Thank you to my readers, old and new, for taking a chance on my books.

You are the reason I write the stories I do. As long as you keep reading, I'll keep writing.

I'm truly humbled by your support and encouragement.

www.ingramcontent.com/pod-product-compliance
Lightning Source LLC
Chambersburg PA
CBHW011750010726
47498CB00012B/3009